...ne creatures were 'haira', pa... ...,
and a bit bigger than Ben's hand. Each one forced its
way, wriggling legs first, through a hole in the grille,
then followed its predecessor, crawling up towards the
ceiling. Their movements were identical and the flow of
them seemed endless. Gaping, Ben walked to the next
pillar along, on the opposite side of the stairs, and saw
another emerging line of creatures just like the first lot –
just as many.

'What . . . ?' he gibbered again. 'What the hell . . . ?'

www.kidsatrandomhouse.co.uk

SAM ENTHOVEN

CRAWLERS

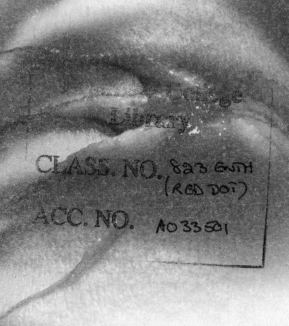

CORGI BOOKS

CRAWLERS
A CORGI BOOK 978 0 552 55870 9

First published in Great Britain by Corgi Books,
an imprint of Random House Children's Books
A Random House Group Company

This edition published 2010

1 3 5 7 9 10 8 6 4 2

The Random House Group Limited supports The Forest Stewardship Council (FSC),
the leading international forest certification organisation. All our titles that are printed
on Greenpeace approved FSC certified paper carry the FSC logo. Our paper
procurement policy can be found at www.rbooks.co.uk/environment

Set in Frutiger Light

Corgi Books are published by Random House Children's Books,
61–63 Uxbridge Road, London W5 5SA

www.**kids**at**randomhouse**.co.uk
www.**rbooks**.co.uk

Addresses for companies within The Random House Group Limited can be found at:
www.randomhouse.co.uk/offices.htm

THE RANDOM HOUSE GROUP Limited Reg. No. 954009

A CIP catalogue record for this book is available from the British Library.

Printed in the UK by CPI Bookmarque, Croydon, CR0 4TD

*To Jack Finney, John Carpenter, H. R. Giger
and Valve Software, with thanks for
some of my very favourite nightmares*

'And soul by soul and silently her
shining bounds increase . . .'

Cecil Spring-Rice
from *I Vow to Thee, My Country*

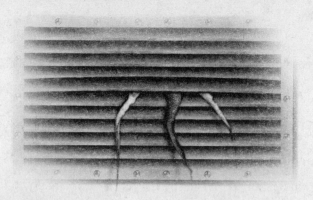

LONDON.
The financial district, aka the City.
Deep underground.

6:16 PM.

In the dark pit that had been my prison for almost three hundred and fifty years, Steadman's latest victim was regaining consciousness.

'Mr Miller?' said Steadman's voice from the pit's wall-mounted speakers. 'Mr Miller? Can you hear me?'

There was a groan. 'Wh . . . what?' The voice was that of a young man, not much more than a teenager. 'Where am I? What . . . what happened?'

'I imagine,' said Steadman, 'that the last thing you remember is lunch at my club. You spent most of the meal boasting about some trivial few million you made on the money markets this morning. For my part, I allowed you to imagine that the Corporation might be interested in you for a

I

purpose other than your present one – and drugged your wine.' He sighed. 'Shocking way to treat a fine Margaux, I know. But then, so was wasting it on you.'

'Mr Steadman,' said his victim, trying for reason, 'Lionel, I don't—'

'Kindly shut up and let me tell you what you're doing there.'

Miller fell silent.

'I . . . hate you,' Steadman began. 'I've never had the chance to say this to one of you before, but I've hated people like you my whole life. Ever since school, where my existence was made a misery by a smug, self-satisfied waster just like you, I have quietly dedicated my life to finding ways to revenge myself on your kind.

'Something unpleasant is about to happen to you. But you can comfort yourself with two things. First, it will be over far more quickly than you deserve, and second, you're in a very privileged position. You, Mr Miller, are about to *serve the Queen*.'

I took my cue.

'*Gah!*' cried Miller into the darkness when I first touched him. 'What's that?'

'What's what?' Steadman asked, amused.

'There's something . . . crawling. Like a spider. It's . . . going up my legs. Now it's on my back! I can't . . . Oh! Oh, *God*! *GET IT OFF ME!*'

Mr Miller shrieked – a short, high note, his voice driven to that pitch by absolute terror.

The shriek stopped.

Then I spoke through his mouth.

'I . . . like this one, Steadman.' The words were husky and thick at first as I worked the unfamiliar vocal cords. 'He's young. Healthy. Much better than the sickly things you usually bring me.'

'A treat for you, my Queen,' said Steadman. 'And he's just the first of many. As of now, you no longer have to make do with those dregs I can steal from the streets without anyone noticing. As of this moment, you can take anyone you want.' He paused, then said: 'You are free.'

Free. More than three centuries had passed while I had been held captive in this pit. In the early days Steadman's predecessors had kept me here with spiked chains and armed guards. Behind those guards had stood more guards, their weapons trained on the first in case I did what I do.

Now, in Mr Steadman's time, I heard an echoing hiss and a whine of machinery. As the lid of my pit drew back I allowed myself a moment of triumph. From that first, blazing night when they caught me I had known this day would come. The reason was simple: they had not killed me. Even in 1666 the Corporation of London had recognized my . . . gifts.

'You accept my offer then, Steadman?' I asked him, through the young man's mouth.

'Not . . . quite.' Even through the speakers on the pit walls I could hear the smile in Steadman's voice.

'To the left of your pit,' he said, 'there is a door. Through it you could go anywhere you want, but the door is shut and the only one who can open it is me. To the right of your pit is a second door: that door is open. It leads to the building above us, a building known as the Barbican. There I've set up . . . a little bet.'

I waited. I had waited a long time. I was patient.

'You've never seen the Barbican, of course,' said Steadman. 'The Corporation completed it in nineteen sixty-nine – rather after your time. Then, it was the largest performing arts centre in Europe. Now . . .' He paused. 'Well, you'll find out.

'I'm giving you a chance to prove yourself, my Queen,' he went on. 'If you show me that you can do what you claim, I'll accept your offer. The first door will open. We'll go through. Together, you and I will take charge of this world and run it the way it should be run.'

'And if I . . . displease you?'

'This room, along with the whole of the Barbican, is rigged with explosives. At midnight precisely they will detonate. The entire building will be destroyed, erasing all evidence of tonight's events – including, if I have not opened the first door, *you*. Do we understand each other?'

'Yes.' I understood him better than he knew.

'Then go, my Queen,' said Steadman. 'You have less than six hours. If you're as powerful as you say, you'll know what to do. And I can hardly wait,' he added, 'to see you do it.'

Already my hands were moving. All of them. The pit resounded with soft, crawling sounds.

My wait was over. Now, at last, I could begin.

LONDON WALL, EC2.

The minibus of the Walsingham School for Boys, approaching the Barbican from the south.

7:18 PM.

Ben Freeman looked out at the passing streets and thought how much he hated his school.

The Walsingham School for Boys was a smart, fee-paying boarding school in Sussex. Ben hated that his days and even his nights there were strictly scripted and timetabled; he hated the school's relentless focus on 'excellence' which, at Walsingham, meant sport, exams or both – and nothing else. But there was a third reason.

Ben was the youngest in his family: he had two older

sisters. He'd grown up in a female-dominated household, so Ben supposed that his parents had sent him to Walsingham in the hope he would make friends with other boys. It was a good theory. Ben's two abiding loves in life – games and horror films – were things his sisters, his mum and lately even his dad all seemed to find somehow regrettable. So when Ben had first arrived at Walsingham the previous term, he had hoped to meet people who shared his tastes – some like-minded guys he could get on with.

Instead, Ben had met the people in the minibus.

'Here's an interesting fact for you, boys . . .' said Mr Clissold.

Each student at Walsingham was put into a small tutor group, looked after by one of the teachers. The idea was to provide a less formal support network outside main school hours, someone the students could go to if they had stuff to discuss. Tutors also organized outings for their groups, like tonight's to the theatre. Mr Clissold, Ben's tutor, had bad breath. Also his definition of 'interesting' wasn't the same as Ben's – or, Ben reckoned, most people's.

'You know that London's divided into boroughs?' said Mr Clissold. 'Well, technically the City *isn't actually one of them.*'

He paused. Ben and the three other boys in the tutor group did not reply.

'It's because of the way the City is run,' Mr Clissold explained, undeterred. 'It's very unusual. Unlike the rest of the country, instead of a local council the City is governed by a special self-appointed body of officials: the Corporation of London.'

'It's been that way for centuries,' said Josh Compton-Smith. 'Isn't that right?'

'That's right, Josh,' said Mr Clissold, surprised. 'Since eleven forty-one, in fact, when—'

'The Corporation's not terribly famous, it's true,' said Josh, 'but it's extremely influential. They own some of the most valuable land and property in the world, including five of London's bridges and most of the City itself. They've got their own special police force – the City of London Police. They've even got a private *power station*, so the City keeps on running no matter what.'

'That's . . .' said Mr Clissold, taking his eyes off the road for a second. 'Actually, Josh, it seems you know more about this subject than I do.'

Josh Compton-Smith gave his most dazzling grin, shrugged and said: 'Of course. My dad works for them.'

Ben rolled his eyes and went back to looking out of the window.

Josh was old for their school year, almost fourteen. He had floppy blond hair, and perfect teeth, and clear skin tanned by expensive holidays. Josh owned the latest gadgets. He was captain of the football team. His exam results were excellent. He even managed to make the school uniform, with its nasty maroon blazer, somehow look good on him. Everyone at Walsingham liked Josh. Everyone, in turn, wanted Josh to like them.

Ben, four months off fourteen himself, was dark-haired, pale and freckled. On Ben's narrow shoulders the maroon jacket looked ridiculous. And Ben thought Josh was an arrogant prick.

BRAAAAAAAAP. The warm air in the minibus was tainted by a pungent waft of semi-digested sausages.

'Hugo,' said Josh mildly.

'Sorry, mate,' said Hugo Walsh, grinning.

Massive, square-headed, broad-shouldered, with bristly red hair, Hugo gave off a constant whiff of body odours of various kinds. He was destined to be an officer in the army, just like his father had been. He was Josh's right-hand man and he loved it, hanging on Josh's words, laughing at his jokes. Hugo himself only had one joke: he didn't tell it with his mouth but he told it again and again, and every time he did, everyone except Ben acted like it was the funniest thing they'd ever heard.

'Mr Walsh,' said Mr Clissold, 'I do believe you produce more greenhouse gases than this minibus.'

'That certainly was a particularly noxious emission, mate,' said Josh with approval – making Hugo's grin widen.

8

'He's a one-man ecological catastrophe!' said Robert Cubbage.

Josh looked at Robert and raised an eyebrow. Hugo's grin froze. The minibus fell silent.

Here we go again, thought Ben.

Robert was still smiling, but in his round, pudgy face his large cow-like eyes were darting about nervously. Robert was young for their year, not much more than thirteen. He was overweight and a bit sweaty. Robert wanted to be accepted. He would do anything to join Hugo and Josh, be part of their team, bask in their glow.

'I do *so* love your accent, Robert,' Josh purred after a moment, once he'd selected which form Robert's humiliation would take this time. 'Let's hear it again: say "photograph".'

Ben watched as Robert started to squirm.

Accents mattered at Walsingham: there was only one acceptable way to speak and any deviation set you apart from the crowd, left you vulnerable. Robert worked harder than most to hide his home accent. It was part of his effort to be accepted. But Josh knew the truth and would never allow Robert or anyone else to forget it.

Robert's smile faltered. 'Photograph,' he said gamely, keeping the 'o's and 'a' long.

'Not like that,' said Josh. 'Say it how you *normally* say it.'

Robert looked at his feet.

Why does Robert put up with this? Ben wondered, watching him. Why did anybody?

'Photograph,' murmured Robert, in his own voice.

'*Footergruff*,' echoed Josh, delighted. 'Have I got that right, Robert? *Footergruff.* You try it, Hugo.'

'Footergruff,' said Hugo, grinning again.

'Footergruff!' said Josh – then sneered. 'It sounds like one of Hugo's farts.'

Ben cleared his throat and said: 'Leave him alone, Josh.'

Josh flinched. 'What did you say?'

'I said,' said Ben, 'leave him alone.'

'Now, boys,' said Mr Clissold nervously from the driving seat. 'There's no need for unpleasantness.'

'None intended, sir,' said Josh, sounding shocked for the teacher's benefit, but staring hard at Ben. 'We were only having a bit of fun. Weren't we, Robert?'

'That's right,' said Robert.

'Ben here just got the wrong end of the stick,' said Josh, with a smile that showed his teeth. 'Didn't you, mate?'

Ben gave Josh an answering smile that was every bit as sincere as Josh had been in calling him 'mate'. But said nothing.

GOSWELL ROAD, EC1.
A London bus, route number 153, approaching the Barbican from the north.

7:21 PM.

An explosion of sound resolved into beats. There was a bar of keyboard intro, made thin and tinny by a mobile phone's built-in speaker. Then Samantha Jackson and Lauren Wallace started to sing.

'OOOOOOOH baby babe . . .' they crooned, grinning at each other as everyone on the bus turned to stare at them.

Ms Gresham, their teacher, gave them a weary look. 'Stop that, you two.'

'OOOOOOOH baby babe,' Samantha and Lauren sang, louder, 'I'm a slave to your love!'

Jasmine Ashworth rested her head against the cool glass of the bus window and sighed.

The Swatham Academy for Girls was a comprehensive in East London. Jasmine, Samantha and Lauren had been students there since they were eleven. Having no minibus was among the least of Swatham's problems: government inspectors had recently put the Academy on what they called 'special measures'. Officially described as 'inadequate' in the inspectors' report, the school had been given one year to show drastic improvement or it would be closed.

'Samantha and Lauren, turn that music off *right now*,' said Ms Gresham.

Ms Gresham was a supply teacher, recently drafted in to Swatham as part of the improvement drive. Jasmine liked her. She was young for a teacher, and with her chic, boyish bob and her smart grey trouser suits she looked good too. Also, unlike some teachers Jasmine could name, Ms Gresham was passionate about her subject – English literature – hence tonight's outing to the theatre. Ms Gresham had a black belt in aikido. She had crossed America on a Harley-Davidson. She had done things with her life. None of that made the slightest difference to Samantha and Lauren.

'Why?' Samantha asked as the tinny beats continued.

'Yeah, miss, what we got to turn it off for?' said Lauren.

'Two reasons,' said Ms Gresham. 'First, you're disturbing the other passengers on this bus. And second, because if you don't, then on Monday you'll both get two hours' detention.'

Jasmine lifted her head from the glass and watched what happened next in the reflection against the darkness outside.

Lauren was pouting – which in Jasmine's opinion was never a good look for her: with Lauren's chubby cheeks, big forehead and squashed nose it tended to make her look even more like a sulky pug dog than she did already. But Lauren wasn't the reason Jasmine didn't want to turn round yet.

Samantha was looking Ms Gresham dead in the eye.

In the three years since they'd all started at Swatham, Samantha had made herself quite a reputation. She had been suspended for fighting no less than three times – once, most memorably, for grabbing another girl by the hair and slamming her face into the edge of a hand basin in the toilets, breaking the girl's nose. To avoid outright expulsion for this incident Samantha had claimed she'd acted in self-defence. Her victim – understandably wary of making Samantha angry again – had backed up her story. Jasmine, and almost everyone else at Swatham, had used the same caution around Samantha ever since.

'I'm not kidding, Samantha,' said Ms Gresham, looking straight back. 'Turn that music off or you'll be sorry.'

Like Jasmine, Samantha was nearly fourteen. Her hard blue eyes and prominent cheekbones gave her a face a narrow, pinched look. Slowly she touched a finger to a loose strand of her bottle-blonde hair, tucking it behind her ear. Then, once she'd made it clear she wasn't being rushed, she dropped her eyes to her phone. The music cut out.

'Miss,' she said, rolling her eyes, 'it's *boring* on this bus, innit.'

'Yeah, miss,' chorused Lauren. 'We've been on here for ages!'

'It's not far now,' said Ms Gresham (though Jasmine thought she sounded every bit as impatient to get there as Samantha and Lauren). 'The curtain goes up at seven forty-five. We should arrive just in time to get to our seats. But right now, we'll just have to pass the time with a little conversation. What shall we talk about?'

No answer.

'How about what you're all going to do when you're older?' said Ms Gresham brightly but with obvious desperation. 'Well? Who wants to start?'

Now Jasmine had another reason to keep looking out of the window. She knew *exactly* what she wanted to do when she was older. But she wasn't about to mention it now.

Jasmine was an only child. Her mother worked shifts at their local supermarket; her father, a musician, had left before Jasmine was born. Jasmine's mum wanted Jasmine to leave school at sixteen, get herself a paying job to help support them both – 'start pulling her weight', as she put it. Obtaining her permission to come to the play tonight had been bad enough; when Jasmine had told her mum about her real ambitions, there had been a row. Her mother had called Jasmine 'a dreaming good-for-nothing like your dad'. But Jasmine knew she wasn't a dreamer. She had *plans*.

She was going to get the best exam results – not just the best her school had learned to tolerate from its pupils but *the best results it was possible to get*. Then she was going to go to the best university, where she would study Earth Sciences. Jasmine would graduate with a top-class degree and soon after that she would realize her ultimate goal: she would become an environmentalist, using her skills and knowledge to change destructive behaviours of governments and industry all over the world.

Jasmine knew what she wanted out of her life. But talking about things like that – even to Ms Gresham – just wasn't what you did around Samantha and Lauren. So she kept looking out of the window, avoiding Ms Gresham's eye.

As she did so, however, Jasmine felt a small pang of guilt. Because if she didn't answer, and Samantha and Lauren stayed silent, then the only person left was . . .

'Lisa,' said Ms Gresham, rounding on the fourth of the students she was taking to the theatre that night. 'What do *you* want to be?'

Through the curtain of lank, mouse-brown hair that she kept over her face at all times, Lisa Staunton darted her teacher a pleading glance. But Ms Gresham was implacable.

'Come on, Lisa,' she coaxed. 'You can tell us.'

'Yeah, Lisa,' said Samantha. 'We're all friends here.' Samantha's voice was sincere. Only the smirk she gave Lauren when Ms Gresham wasn't looking told the truth.

Jasmine turned to watch.

Lisa Staunton was a mystery to her. Ever since their first day at Swatham Lisa had slipped instantly into the role of school victim and underdog – and stayed there. Samantha and Lauren barely bothered to mock Lisa to her face any more. Instead, she had become a kind of Swatham catchphrase: if, say, an elbow of your school blazer was wearing through, you could say it had 'gone a bit Lisa' and everyone would know what you meant. Lisa's much-mended clothes were the stuff of school legend, together with her spots, her overbite, her total lack of friends and a host of other attributes, real and imagined.

But despite the fact that Lisa was treated so cruelly, Jasmine sometimes wondered if she didn't secretly somehow *like* it that way. She did nothing to defend herself. Her default reaction to everything was simply to sit there, shoulders hunched, hair over her face, silent, passive. She was doing it now.

'What were your ambitions when you were little?' asked Ms Gresham. 'What would you most love to do, Lisa? What are your dreams?'

For another moment Lisa didn't answer – just quivered slightly like a cornered animal. She blinked her watery eyes very rapidly several times, then, to everyone's astonishment, said: 'I used to want to be a ballerina.'

The four girls and their teacher shared a short silence.

Then Samantha and Lauren burst into hoots of laughter.

'What's so funny, you two?' asked Ms Gresham, annoyed.

Jasmine sighed. It was going to be a long evening.

THE BARBICAN CENTRE.
The main entrance on Silk Street.

7:35 PM.

The lights of the entranceway were dazzling after the darkness outside. Ben followed Mr Clissold and the maroon-jacketed backs of the other boys down a white-walled, fridge-bright passage. Automatic glass-panelled doors slid back and the Barbican opened around him.

Ben looked up, surprised. At the time it was built the Barbican was probably supposed to look smart and futuristic. It didn't any more: to Ben, it just looked weird. The proportions were boxy and lumpish, the lights low and gloomy. The carpet beneath his feet was an unappealing mud-grey with what looked like thousands of blue worms trampled into it for a pattern, and almost everything else he could see was made out of concrete, spattered with small embedded stones, giving the walls the texture of lumpy porridge. Beyond the black open counter that served as the Barbican's box office the foyer splintered into a confusing array of walkways and stairs that led in contrary directions, like something out of an Escher print.

The Barbican, thought Ben, *looks like it was designed by a kid.*

'Hi!' said a voice, interrupting his reverie. Ben looked down: a man had come out from behind the counter. He was dressed all in dark blue with an orange armband. He had an unfeasible gelled blond hairdo and an equally unfeasible smile: his eyes looked oddly glassy and blank.

'I'm Jeremy,' he said. 'Welcome to the Barbican. This way, please.'

'Jeremy' led the group along a walkway, down two flights of stairs that were carpeted in the same horrible pattern, and finally held open some double doors off to one side of the foyer's lower level.

Suddenly Ben and his tutor group were in the stalls of the Main Theatre. The auditorium and its upper balconies were a good size and mostly full; the noise of over a thousand people chatting and settling into their seats swelled around Ben as he followed the group along to their row. He had been to big theatres before, so this didn't faze him.

Ben realized he was going to be sitting next to Robert. To his surprise, Robert was smiling at him.

'Thanks, Ben,' he murmured as Ben sat.

'What for?'

Robert's smile faded a little, but he leaned closer to Ben. 'For . . . you know, sticking up for me.'

Mr Clissold had sat down on Robert's left, in the middle of the group; Hugo and Josh were beyond him, almost certainly out of earshot, what with the surrounding noise of the rest of the audience. But Robert obviously felt he was taking a big risk in saying what he had. Ben figured he'd better say something back.

He shrugged. He opened his mouth. He got as far as: 'It was noth—'

Then an ice cream landed on his head.

The sensation was very cold and very sudden, and at first Ben was uncertain what had actually happened. As he groped in his sticky hair to find out, a chilly dribble of vanilla ran down the side of his neck. He looked up, and his eyes met those of a girl sitting above him, at the front of the circle.

The girl was about his age, and she was *gorgeous*. Her skin was the colour of melting chocolate. Her large and beautiful dark brown eyes stared straight down into his. Her lips, even pursed in deep annoyance as they were, filled Ben's mind with sudden and distracting thoughts of kisses. Ice cream on his head or no, he couldn't take his eyes off her.

The girl looked along her row. At the spot directly above where Ben had been sitting, something was happening.

7:47 PM.

'That's it,' said Ms Gresham. 'Everyone outside.'

'But, miss,' said Samantha, blue eyes glinting, 'you've got to admit it was a good shot.'

'Right on his head!' said Lauren. 'Genius!'

'Get . . .' repeated Ms Gresham, in a tight voice Jasmine had never heard her use before, '*out*. All of you. Now.'

Samantha touched her bottle-blonde mane above her right ear and smiled. 'Fine,' she said. 'We didn't want to see your stupid play anyway.' She turned to Lauren. 'Come on, babes, we're going.'

Grinning, Lauren followed her mistress. Lisa got up and meekly went after them.

Jasmine scowled.

She made it out of the row of muttering, disapproving theatre-goers just as the lights were going down. The performance was about to start – and, in the passageway beyond the doors, so was the one from Ms Gresham. She wasn't the first teacher Samantha had pushed to the limit. *Here we go again*, Jasmine thought.

'I am *so* disappointed in you girls,' Ms Gresham said as the doors closed behind her. 'You four were the only ones in the class whose parents even deigned to give their permission for you to come on this trip. The journey was a nightmare but we get here at last, I buy you all a treat to make the most of the occasion, and what happens? You have to go and ruin it.' She looked around the group. 'I just don't know what to do with you. Don't you want to take something from your education? Don't you *want* the chance to make something of yourselves? Because if not, I'm sorry to say I'm starting to wonder why I should bother with you.'

Samantha let that hang in the air for a moment, shrugged, then said, 'Great. Don't. See if we care.'

'Hah!' said Lauren as Samantha turned to receive the high five she already had waiting.

Ms Gresham went very pale.

Jasmine put her hand up. 'Miss?'

'Yes, Jasmine?'

'Miss, are we going back in to watch the play?'

'No, Jasmine,' said Ms Gresham. 'It seems I can't take you girls anywhere without you making a nuisance of yourselves. So we're going home.'

Jasmine did not reply. It was as she'd expected.

The play they'd been about to see was Shakespeare's *Henry IV Part 1*. Unlike perhaps anyone else at her school, Jasmine had read it. The play was going to be one of the set texts for their exams at the end of the year. English literature wasn't Jasmine's best subject – in fact it was her weakest – but she needed a full set of first-class exam results to get her plans started and prove to her mother that she was serious. Seeing the play could really have helped, particularly since she'd never actually seen one performed professionally before.

Jasmine had thought Ms Gresham was different, strong enough to stand up to Samantha – or at least to see past her and realize that not everyone at Swatham was the same. But no: once again it was 'you girls'. In minutes now, Jasmine thought, they would be back on the bus, leaving another missed opportunity behind them.

She was wrong.

7:52 PM.

There. Ben's maroon school jacket was going to need a visit to the dry cleaner's and he was giving off a strong whiff of vanilla, but at least he'd managed to get the worst of the goop out of his hair. He took his head out from under the hand-dryer and looked in the mirror.

He was standing, alone, in a gents' toilet on the Barbican foyer's lower level – the nearest washing facilities he'd been able to find after his dripping and ignominious exit from the theatre. The yellow-shaded fluorescent strip lights buzzed overhead, flickering.

Look at this place, Ben thought. Even the toilet walls were made of concrete – great panels of it, looming inwards, making the space seem narrow and claustrophobic. What with this and the impressions he'd had of the rest of the Barbican so far – the pulsating carpet, the empty corridors deadened into silence now the performance was underway – the whole situation was beginning to remind Ben of something. It took him a while to work out what, but when he did, he forgot about the ice cream and smiled.

Games. The place reminded him of games: specifically, old-school first person shooters – the ones where you're running down corridors and being attacked by monsters. That was what walking around the Barbican felt like. Ben's grin widened as he let his imagination run with the idea.

If this was a game, your classic survival horror type, the room he was standing in would have a monster in it. Something or someone would be lurking in the cubicles, would crash through the door or drop from the ceiling and try to eat his face, or—

His grin froze. The washbasin mirror was wide: in the corner of the reflection in front of him he'd seen movement.

Ben turned. He stared. He blinked. But he saw nothing.

Idiot, he told himself. He turned, pushed open the heavy swing door and stepped out, his thoughts going back to the gorgeous girl in the theatre.

Behind him, something moved again.

7:54 PM.

'Excuse me,' said Ms Gresham to the Barbican security man. 'Hello?'

The guard's glassy stare swung and locked. 'No way out,' he said.

'Yes, thank you,' said Ms Gresham, 'that's what the man at the main entrance said too. But which way *is* the way out, please?'

The security man didn't move. He just stood there, arms folded, in front of the glass door. 'No way out,' he repeated dully.

After a couple of false starts – the way wasn't straight forward – Jasmine's group had found a walkway down from the upper circle to the ground floor of the Barbican's foyer. But as they did so, Jasmine had noticed something strange. The building's staff, in their orange armbands, had gathered from all areas of the complex. None of them spoke. Their radios remained on their belts. But they spread out wordlessly around the foyer's edges. Keys were inserted. Glass-panelled doors were locked shut. For good measure, the staff then stood in front of the doors, each one assuming the same position as the security guard: arms folded, glassy eyes staring emptily.

One by one, Jasmine realized, all the exits were being

blocked. For some reason it appeared that the Barbican's staff wanted to keep everyone from leaving.

What was going on?

7:56 PM.

'What the hell . . . ?' said Ben, aloud. He was standing at the bottom of the stairs on the lower level of the foyer. He'd been on his way back to the theatre when his attention had been caught by the nearest of the massive, grey, square concrete pillars that bestrode the room like giants' legs.

Halfway up each pillar an oval grille had been punched into the concrete. These metal-slatted vents stared out into the room like black, lidless eyes. And something was coming out of them.

For a second Ben was reminded of a nature documentary he'd seen once about worker ants – columns of them, marching unstoppably over every obstacle. With a tingle he realized that what he was seeing was something similar.

A long line of spider-like creatures was emerging from the foyer's air-vents. The creatures were hairless, pale, rubbery-looking, and a bit bigger than Ben's hand. Each one forced its way, wriggling legs first, through a hole in the grille, then followed its predecessor, crawling up towards the ceiling. Their movements were identical and the flow of them seemed endless. Gaping, Ben walked to the next pillar along, on the opposite side of the stairs, and saw another emerging line of creatures just like the first lot – just as many.

'What . . . ?' he gibbered again. 'What the hell . . . ?'

An alarm bell rang.

'Attention, ladies and gentlemen,' boomed a voice from loudspeakers all over the building. *'This is an emergency. This evening's performances are cancelled. The building is being evacuated. Please make your way to the upper level of the foyer.'*

Ben looked around the foyer's still-empty lower level. The sudden alarm had made him jump: his heart was beating fast and a sick taste was climbing the back of his throat. For a moment he wasn't sure what to do.

'Ladies and gentlemen, please make your way to the upper level of the foyer as quickly as possible. This is not a drill.' The voice carried on, repeating its instructions again and again.

The theatre doors slapped back on their hinges and the first people came through. Chatting loudly, a rapidly thickening snake of theatre-goers milled past Ben, doing what they were told and heading up the stairs. So far the crowd were all adults – ordinary men and women dressed in jackets and coats and cardigans. Some of them looked annoyed. Some looked disbelieving. Most looked confused and more than a little panicky. Ben didn't want to have to explain what he was doing there and why he wasn't moving, so he didn't meet their eyes. Instead he looked up at the pillars again – but the strange creatures seemed to have gone. He was still searching for any sign of them when—

'Freeman!'

It was Josh, using Ben's surname. Ben turned and saw that Mr Clissold and the tutor group were just coming out of the theatre. By now the crowd going up the stairs was forcing Ben to shrink back against the railing to avoid being swept along with them. He knew that it would probably have been a mistake to stay on his own, but as he watched Josh and the others make their way towards him, a part of him wished he hadn't waited.

'Right,' said Mr Clissold as they reached him. 'Now at least we've got everybody. Well then, until we find out what this is all about I suppose you'd better follow me.'

The mass of jostling people pulled the group along. The pressure of the crowd was irresistible, the staircase narrowing and squeezing them on like toothpaste out of a tube.

'Um, sir . . . ?' said Ben. Even if the crawling things hadn't vanished it would have been hard to make anyone believe him, but he had to say something. 'When I went to the loo, I saw something weird.'

'Not now, Ben,' said Mr Clissold.

Hugo made a snorting noise in his nose. Josh just smirked – and perhaps, Ben reflected, that hadn't been the best way to put it. Ignoring a sympathetic if nervous look from Robert, he gritted his teeth.

Forward progress was getting slower. The upper level was rapidly becoming packed with bodies. The Main Theatre must have emptied completely by now, along with the Barbican's concert hall, cinemas, and the rest of it. But there was nowhere for the crowd to go. Moments ago there had been silence and emptiness; now there were people everywhere, and they were getting anxious. Individual voices merged into the swelling crush as the crowd took on a life of its own, becoming something less than human. The noise was getting louder and the room was getting hotter.

Ben looked up at the ceiling.

8:03 pm.

Jasmine hated crowds. It was partly her height: for her, being in a crowd usually meant getting a faceful of some stranger's armpit. But worse even than that was the loss of control, the helplessness. Jasmine hated feeling powerless, hated it more than anything, but she felt it now: her arms were pressed to her sides; the room was so tightly packed that moving at all was an effort. As the people around her surged and shoved all she could do was sway with the rest and try to keep her feet.

'It's all right, girls,' said Ms Gresham from beside her. 'It's all going to be all right.'

Jasmine looked at her teacher. If this was Ms Gresham's best effort to reassure them, it wasn't working. In fact it just made things worse: something was wrong here, badly wrong, Jasmine knew it. She stood on tiptoe, craned her neck and looked over at the Barbican's main entrance. Six angry people in Shakespearean costume – actors from the play – were arguing with glassy-eyed Barbican staff there and meeting with just as little response as Ms Gresham had.

'Someone must have known about the alarm,' said Jasmine, thinking aloud. 'Why did they lock the doors? Why won't they let us out?'

'We're trapped here,' said Samantha.

'What're you talking about, trapped here?' asked Lauren, her voice rising. 'Why would we be trapped here?'

'Calm down, Lauren,' said Ms Gresham. 'And Samantha, I'd appreciate it if you'd keep observations like that to yourself. This will all be over in a moment, I'm sure.'

Still on tiptoe, Jasmine craned her head round as best she could, looking for clues about what was going on.

There! She saw a flash of movement out of the corner of her eye: something had dropped from above to land in the crowd.

The hubbub was pierced by a scream.

Jasmine's eye was caught by another falling object, closer this time, over to her left. Now more were falling, and more, until the objects were dropping all over the room.

More screams. Jasmine felt the crowd crush in around her, flinching as one.

'What's happening?' a woman next to her was saying, her voice high and shrill. 'What are they trying to get away from? *Why won't anyone tell me what's—?*'

Then, unbelievably, the whole ceiling seemed to fall in.

Ben ducked, instinctively throwing his arms up over his head. But the impact when it came wasn't like a ceiling collapse; it was more like . . . what? The touch on his head was light, scrabbling, ticklish. Shuddering, Ben batted it away hard without thinking. He straightened up, opened his eyes, and saw pandemonium.

All over the foyer people seemed to have gone into some sort of dancing frenzy – twisting, slapping at themselves, waving their arms about. '*Get it off me!*' roared Mr Clissold, crashing into him and almost knocking him over. '*Get it off! AAAAAGH!*'

Ben's eyes went wide.

One of the crawling creatures he'd seen earlier was on Mr Clissold's back. Quickly but very deliberately it made its way up the centre of his spine, out of reach of his slapping hands. Now it was between his shoulder blades. It waited there a moment, reared up on its rubbery legs and then, before Ben could do anything more than gape, it clamped itself to the back of Mr Clissold's neck.

Mr Clissold went rigid. His eyes rolled back. Then he fell to the ground.

Ben stared at his teacher's prone body for a moment, blinking, unable to process what he was seeing. Then suddenly he noticed space all around him: the pressure of the crowd was gone. This, he realized, was for the simple reason that what had happened to Mr Clissold was happening to others too.

Everywhere people were screaming, going rigid and falling to the floor.

'*Aaaaaaah!*' Jasmine was shrieking like a banshee. She couldn't help it. Some kind of horrible spider had dropped from the ceiling and was clinging to her stomach. She tried to brush it away: there was a repulsive sticky sensation on the side of her hand where she made contact with it, but the creature just clung on stubbornly. It reared up. Jasmine slapped at it again, and this time she dislodged it. But as the creature hit the floor it righted itself, dodged left, climbed her leg, and now it was crawling up her back.

Jasmine froze to the spot, frantic with horror and disgust. As it climbed, she could feel the tips of its feet through the material of her school bl—

The blazer. Jasmine grabbed her lapels and yanked the jacket off. Ripping her arms out of the sleeves, with trembling fingers she threw it down on the floor.

Still the creature was undeterred. Jasmine watched as first one then the rest of its scrabbling limbs found their way out from underneath the cloth. It was coming for her again. In another second it was going to jump up her legs again, but this time—

RUTCH!

The pointed tip of an umbrella speared it where it stood. Its legs quivered for a moment, then went still.

'Yuck,' said Ms Gresham. She pulled the umbrella out of the creature's body and wiped the prong on the side of her shoe with a grimace.

'What . . . ?' gasped Jasmine. 'What *is* that thing, miss?'

'Right now I suggest we don't hang around to find out,' said Ms Gresham. 'We'll try for the lifts. Everyone follow me!'

As Jasmine scrambled after Ms Gresham she saw a blur of horrors: shrieking faces; bulging eyes; kicking legs. Everywhere she looked there were the wriggling movements of more of the creatures – on torsos, in hair, scampering over mouths and ears and nostrils. Jasmine glimpsed all this but there was no time to take it in; that would come later, when her mind would play everything back to her in full and excruciating detail. For now she was like an animal, her whole being stripped down to the most primal response there is. For now, Jasmine just ran for her life.

'This way!' Ms Gresham shouted, holding the door as Jasmine piled into the metal cubicle, behind Samantha and Lauren. 'And you!' she added. 'You boys! Come on – in here!'

The voice snapped Ben out of his paralysis. He saw the lift with the lady outside it – the one sheltered spot in the room – and he ran for it.

At the threshold he hesitated. The lift was small, perhaps only a couple of metres square, and already packed with people. But hands shoved him on and more bodies squashed in behind him.

'Let's go, miss!' said a girl's voice. 'Come on! Let's get out of here!'

The lady teacher shepherded in one more student (a girl with her hair over her eyes, Ben noticed) before finally forcing her way in herself. The hot crush of bodies in the lift became tighter still.

'All right,' she said. 'Whoever can reach it, press the button for Level Two. There's another exit with a walkway to street level there, I think.'

'*Doors closing*,' said a recorded female voice. With agonizing slowness the lift's metal panels slid shut.

The screams from outside were muffled.

Silence.

Ben looked around numbly. They had lost Mr Clissold, but he realized that the rest of the tutor group, amazingly, was still intact: it had been Josh and Hugo who had shoved him into the lift, and white-faced Robert's finger was still on its control panel. As well as the lady teacher there were four girls in the lift too. One of them wasn't wearing her blazer any more, but even after the madness of the previous few minutes Ben had no trouble recognizing the beautiful girl from earlier. Then any further thoughts he might have had were abruptly interrupted.

Lauren's lower lip wobbled, her eyes squeezed shut, she threw back her head and she wailed.

Jasmine stared at her. The noise Lauren was making was like the scream of a baby – a rising cry of anguished complaint that bounced around the tiny metal cubicle, setting everyone's teeth on edge.

'Calm down, Lauren,' said Ms Gresham. 'Will you calm down, please?'

Purple-faced, Lauren just drew breath and wailed again.

'She's claustrophobic, miss,' said Samantha helpfully, over the din. 'She can't stand small spaces. She just freaks out completely.'

Jasmine realized they had more pressing things to worry about. 'Miss,' she asked, 'why aren't we moving?'

'*Maximum safe weight limit exceeded,*' said the female voice from the lift's speakers. The voice was rich and musical, and probably intended to have a calming effect on its audience. '*Maximum safe weight limit exceeded,*' it repeated – doing the opposite. '*Doors opening . . .*'

'No, no, no!' said someone. Ben was surprised to find it was himself.

'Hold the door, Robert!' barked Josh. 'Hit the button, Robert, quick!'

Robert jabbed at the panel frantically. The doors ground to a halt halfway across.

A big, bespectacled, balding man dressed in black thrust his stricken face in through the gap. 'Let me in!' he shouted, hammering on the outside of the metal. 'You've got to let me in! They're right behind me! They're—!'

The man went rigid. His eyes rolled up in his head; for a second only the whites were visible before he fell back out of sight. The doors closed again.

Now Lauren wasn't the only one making a noise: everybody in the lift was shouting, swearing, yelling, screaming.

'Quiet,' said Ms Gresham. 'Quiet!' She was a good teacher: when she wanted quiet she got it – even, for the moment, from Lauren. 'Listen,' she said.

'*Maximum safe weight limit exceeded,*' the lift's recorded voice repeated. '*Maximum safe weight limit exceeded. Maximum safe weight limit exc—*'

'There are too many of us in here,' said Ms Gresham. 'I think . . .' She paused. 'I think one of us is going to have to get out.'

Everyone stared at her. The dreadful truth of her words sank in straight away. The lift was not going to move with the number of people currently inside it. To lighten the load and save the others, someone would have to be sacrificed.

But that wasn't their only problem.

Ms Gresham frowned. 'Did one of you touch my foot?' she asked. 'I . . . felt something.'

No one answered.

Ms Gresham blinked. 'Now it's on my leg. None of you are nudging me by mistake, are you? Because . . .'

She trailed off. Her eyes filled with a kind of hopeless horror. 'Now, nobody *panic*,' she said. 'But I'm rather afraid one of those . . . *things* has made it into the lift with us.'

Her last few words were drowned out by moans and

screams from the lift's other occupants. The little metal cubicle had been crammed and claustrophobic enough already; now, as everyone inside it struggled and shoved, madly trying to get away but with nowhere to go, it became intolerable.

'It's on my back,' said Ms Gresham, into the rising pandemonium. 'If we can get it on the floor maybe we can stamp on it. I can't reach! Can't one of you get it off me? It's under my jacket. Now it's under my collar. It's . . . *For God's sake, someone help me!*'

Jasmine saw the pale, eager legs emerge at the nape of her teacher's neck, touching the short hairs there. But Jasmine's arms were pressed against her sides by the crush. She was powerless.

Ms Gresham went rigid, then limp. The press of people in the lift was so tight that there was nowhere for her to fall: she just stayed there, head lolling, with the creature clamped to the back of her neck.

Everyone just stared at her, too horrified to make a sound. For several seconds the silence was broken only by the machine-voice uselessly repeating its message: '*Maximum safe weight limit exceeded. Maximum safe weight limit exceeded.*'

Then the teacher twitched. Her chin lifted from her chest. Her head, still with the creature attached to it, came upright on her shoulders. Her eyelids trembled, then opened. Slowly, as if with great effort, she turned to face Robert and fixed him with a glassy stare.

'*Open the door.*' The voice that came from her mouth sounded harsh, guttural – not at all like it had before.

'I – I'm sorry?' stammered Robert.

A scowl crossed the teacher's brow. Wrenching one arm free from the surrounding crush of bodies, she reached across and took hold of Robert's wrist.

'*Open the door!*' she roared.

'She's . . .' said Robert, hardly able to believe it. 'She's pulling my finger off the door button!'

'*Doors opening . . .*' the recorded voice intoned mercilessly as they slid apart again.

For a frozen moment Jasmine stared out at the scene beyond.

She saw heads and shoulders of an army of what had been ordinary adults crowding at the door. She saw a forest of hands reaching in. She saw eyes: glassy, mindless, staring, their pupils like bottomless black pits.

Then:

'*Gaaaaaaaaaaah!*'

Jasmine turned and glimpsed a flash of blonde hair as Samantha slammed into Ms Gresham – and shoved her out.

The forest of hands grasped the teacher and bore her out of sight. The army of staring adults fell back for a moment. Samantha teetered on the grooves that marked the lift's boundary. Hugo grabbed her. Robert hammered the button.

'*Doors closing*,' said the voice again – and then, at last, '*Going up.*'

8:09 PM.

'Less than four hours left now, my Queen.'

Steadman's sudden voice from the pit's wall-mounted speakers almost broke my concentration.

'Three hours and fifty-one minutes, to be precise,' he added unnecessarily. 'What's your situation?'

'I now control the Barbican,' I said aloud, through the young man's mouth. 'I took the staff first: I used them to seal the exits, then drove everyone else into the foyer, where—'

'I know,' said Steadman.

'You . . . know?' In the darkness of my pit I waited, puzzled.

'You are surprised, my Queen?' said Steadman. 'You thought I would let you loose without keeping an eye on you?' He chuckled drily. 'What you've achieved so far is . . . promising. One begins to see why the Corporation felt driven to do what it did to stop you in sixteen sixty-six. But we are stronger now. I have eyes everywhere. *I am watching you* – never forget it.

'Besides which,' he went on, 'you are mistaken. You do not, in fact, control *everyone* in the Barbican. Right now, at this moment, I can see that eight . . . children' – he said the word with disgust – 'are escaping from the foyer in one of the elevators.'

My turn: 'I know.'

There was a short silence, during which my brief satisfaction at giving Steadman a taste of his own medicine was somewhat spoiled by the knowledge that I was still utterly at his mercy. If he chose to end his 'bet' now, he could simply leave. The Barbican was a deathtrap, and I would die his prisoner.

'Well,' said Steadman, 'I've taken steps to ensure they can't call for help. What I want to know is, what are *you* going to do about them?'

'The children have not escaped, Steadman,' I explained. 'I too now have eyes all over the building – including,' I added, 'in that lift. Everything is under my control.'

'We'll know by midnight,' was Steadman's answer.

8:13 PM.

'Level Two,' said the voice. *'Doors opening . . .'*

The group braced themselves for fresh horror as the doors slid back.

Nobody there. Nothing moving. Silence.

'Right,' said Josh in his best take-charge voice. 'Everybody follow me as quickly and as quietly as you possibly can.'

They stepped out of the lift and onto a landing.

As elsewhere in the building, the walls of the corridor in which the group were now standing were made of concrete – grey and rough and harsh-looking. But the patterned carpet of the foyer had given way to a brick floor, smoothed to a ceramic sheen. Every footstep anyone took sent an echoing clopping sound into the surrounding silence. This made Ben feel very exposed and vulnerable, so to dispel the feeling he tried to occupy his brain by re-counting the people in the group.

There were eight of them now. Four boys. Four girls. No adults.

'Now what?' asked the blonde girl – the one who'd pushed the teacher out of the lift. She stepped forward and looked straight into Josh's eyes.

'We look for that way out your teacher mentioned,' said Josh. He looked back. 'All right?'

After a pause to show that Josh's leadership was strictly temporary, Samantha nodded.

As they set off down the corridor, Jasmine looked around the group to see how everyone was doing. Though no one seemed hurt, they were all very pale. Lauren's lower lip was trembling again, and the eyes of one of the boys looked dangerously watery. Jasmine couldn't blame them: she wasn't feeling too solid herself. The group's current superficial quiet was not going to last.

They came to a security gate. Beyond it were wooden double doors with a green EXIT sign above them. Through the doors' glass portholes they could see another concrete walkway, with open night sky at its far end. But the way to the doors was barred by the security gate. It was the exact height and width of the passage and made of black painted metal. Samantha strode forward and kicked it: the resounding *bang* made everyone wince, but of course it didn't budge.

There was a pause.

'Does that mean we're stuck here?' Robert asked. 'Does that mean . . . we can't get out?'

'I don't know, Robert,' said Ben patiently. 'It's starting to look that way. Yes.'

'But . . . those spider-things,' said Robert, 'and the people downstairs – they might come up here and—'

'Shut up, fat boy,' said Samantha. 'We need to think.'

Robert's face reddened. Sticky tears began to run down his cheeks.

Samantha strikes again, thought Jasmine. She took a deep breath. 'Who's got a phone?'

The whole group stared at her blankly.

'Mine was in my blazer,' said Jasmine, keeping her voice level. 'So which one of us is going to call for help? Come on, it's a simple question.'

The girls snapped out of their trance and began to pat pockets.

'No signal,' said Samantha. 'Haven't had one since we got here.'

Lauren shut her useless mobile and shook her head; Lisa too. Jasmine turned to Josh and looked at him enquiringly.

'Oh,' said Josh blithely, 'we're not allowed mobiles at our school.'

Jasmine blinked. Not having a working phone wasn't something to be casual about: unless they got lucky and found a landline, they had no way of calling for help.

'All right, next question,' she said. 'Does anyone actually *know* any other ways out of here?'

No one answered.

'Then,' said Jasmine firmly, 'we need to find somewhere to hide. Quickly too. We don't know how long we're going to be alone up here.'

'She's right,' said Ben, stepping forward. 'We should find ourselves somewhere safe, somewhere we can defend if we have to. We need time to regroup.'

Josh raised his eyebrows. '"Regroup"?' he echoed. 'And

what makes *you* an expert all of a sudden, Freeman?'

Ben, to his annoyance, felt himself go red. 'Zombie films,' he admitted.

'*What?*' said Samantha, though everyone had heard him perfectly.

'I got it from zombie films.'

Ben wasn't proud or anything. But at that point, thinking about horror films and games seemed like the only way to get a handle on the situation.

'It's good thinking,' said Jasmine. 'Look at us: we're in shock, we don't know what's going on. If we keep moving without knowing where we're going we just risk getting caught out in the open.'

'No,' said Josh. 'Sorry, but I think that if we keep moving we'll have the best chance of finding a way out of here before anything worse happens.'

'Anyway,' said Samantha, 'where exactly were you planning on taking us, *Jasmine*?'

Jasmine sucked her teeth. Samantha had probably only chimed in to make herself look important. But now Jasmine was supposed to produce a plan out of thin air. While the rest of the group looked at her expectantly – the boys as well as the girls – her eyes flicked around the passageway.

'There,' she said, pointing. 'That's what we need: a bit of that, right there.'

The rest of the group turned to see what she was seeing.

Up the passage was a door to the right. It had a sign on it. SECURITY.

Samantha sneered, but—

'All right,' said Josh. 'Let's check it out, at least.'

8:21 PM

The door wasn't locked – that was their first piece of luck. And when the overhead strip lights flickered and blinked into action to reveal a room that was apparently empty of crawling things or any other horrors, that was their second.

The room the group were standing in now was about four metres long by three wide. With all eight of them in there it was perhaps a little more crowded than it had been designed to be, but there were chairs and plenty of floor-space. One wall was covered by a row of metal lockers, presumably used by Barbican staff for their street clothes and personal items. Another wall held a small kitchen worktop with a sink, a kettle, and a cupboard that might contain tea and coffee and other supplies. On the right of where they'd come in was a second door, that led to . . .

'Oh!' said Josh.

Flickering on the wall of the second, smaller room was a grid of monitor screens. It was a display of the feed from the closed circuit security cameras dotted throughout the whole of the Barbican complex.

Josh reached forward and tapped a monitor. 'That looks like a view of the passage outside. Hugo, are you all right to watch the screens?'

'Er, sure, Josh,' said Hugo, blinking but eager. 'No worries, mate. Yeah.'

Josh turned to Jasmine and unleashed one of his devastating smiles. 'Then I think the rest of us could use a cup of tea.'

Jasmine didn't smile back. If this boy was expecting *her* to make tea, then what he was going to get was a slap. But a rising hiss from next door indicated that the kettle was already heating up. Josh turned and went back to the main room: the moment had passed, so Jasmine followed him.

It was a grim scene that greeted her. Apart from the kettle, the security room was silent. No one was looking at anyone else. Everyone was just sitting or standing there. Even Samantha seemed lost in her own private head-space, vainly trying to process the events of the previous half-hour.

'Right,' Josh interrupted brightly. 'It looks like we're all in this together for now, so why don't we introduce ourselves? My name's Josh. Josh Compton-Smith. Let's go round the room.' He turned to Jasmine, smiling again in a prompting way.

'Jasmine,' said Jasmine, who was beginning to dislike Josh.

'I'm Ben,' put in Ben. He didn't like Josh's big 'let's be friends' routine either, but he didn't mind taking his turn now Jasmine had spoken. *Nice name*, he thought, looking at her.

'R-Robert,' stammered a voice from the chair beside him.

'Lisa.' Lisa's voice was quiet and breathy. She'd been the last one into the lift, and now she sat hugging her knees, her long mousey hair like a curtain over her face.

There was a pause. Everyone in the room look expectantly at the next person along, who sneered then shrugged. 'Samantha.'

'Lauren,' said Lauren instantly.

'The bloke watching the screens is called Hugo. Great,' said Josh, nodding. 'Great. Well, now we all know each other's names, we can try and figure out what's going on. Who wants to start?'

The kettle, ignored, clicked off and sputtered back to silence. To Jasmine's complete lack of surprise, it was Samantha who spoke first.

'Is that some kind of trick question, or what?'

'How do you mean?' asked Josh.

'We know what's going on. First we couldn't get out. Then spiders came down from the ceiling and started biting everybody, and *then,* oh yeah, all the people they bit suddenly got up and started going mental – remember?' Samantha rolled her eyes, then looked at Lauren to back her up.

Lauren smirked nervously but obediently.

'That's true,' said Josh. 'But what we need to think about is *why*. Let's start with your first point: why couldn't we get out?'

'The building staff locked the doors,' said Jasmine.

'You saw them do it?'

'Yeah.'

'Interesting,' said Josh. 'And what does that suggest to you?'

Jasmine blinked. 'They knew what was going to happen. They wanted everyone to be stuck in one place.'

'It was a trap,' Ben put in. Everyone looked at him. 'While I was out of the theatre, getting the *ice cream* off my jacket' – he paused to give Samantha a look but he might as well not have bothered: she ignored him – 'I saw those things crawling out of the air-vents in the walls.' He shuddered. 'There were thousands of them.'

'Why didn't you tell anyone?' asked Josh, annoyed.

'I tried,' Ben shot back. 'You didn't listen. Besides, if you hadn't seen it for yourself, would you have believed me? I mean,' Ben went on, his voice rising, 'can anyone believe this stuff is happening to us? It's like a game or something!'

'Come on, mate,' said Josh. 'Let's try and keep calm about this, eh?'

'Calm?' echoed Samantha. '*Calm?* I don't know if they teach you how to deal with situations like this at your school, Posh, but they didn't tell us anything at ours. There are killer spiders coming out of the walls! What good is standing around talking about it going to do?'

'It's *Josh*,' said Josh, 'actually.'

Samantha smirked. 'Like I said: *Posh*. And who put you in charge, anyway?'

'Where did the spider-things come from?' asked Jasmine.

'What's the deal when they bite you?' asked Ben.

'How can we get help?' asked Robert.

'*When do we get out?*' wailed Lauren.

'*Quiet!*' yelled Josh. 'Hugo, what did you say?'

'Sorry, mate,' said Hugo from the doorway to the monitor room, 'but I think they know we're in here.'

8:32 PM.

Jasmine had to crane over to see past Hugo, but a glance at the screen showing the passage outside was all it took. Last time she'd seen it, it had been empty. Now it was full. While they'd been talking, a large group of adults had massed outside. Their eyes were open and staring. They advanced towards the door with an eerie sense of purpose, all at the same time: the fact that the image came without sound made it look like some nightmarish game of Grandmother's Footsteps.

The sudden silence in the room was broken by a low scratching sound.

'The door,' said Robert. 'There's someone at the door!'

The doorknob was turning.

'Use the lockers!' yelled Jasmine.

Ben was already moving. He had pulled one set of lockers away from the wall, and with Hugo's help he was heaving them round to make a barricade. Not a moment too soon: the door was just opening as the lockers were shoved into place, slamming it shut.

A thunderous pounding of fists and feet now came from behind the door and wall. Jasmine stared at the screen. Out there, a crowd of formerly polite, cultured adults were now frenziedly trying to punch and shove and kick their way in. A scrum of them had formed at the door, battering away at it. In response – with a ringing *crash* – Hugo and Ben shored up their first barricade with a second set of lockers. At this, as if on command, the crowd outside suddenly stopped their onslaught. Their hands fell to their sides, and they stood there, frozen.

Silence.

'What are they doing?' whispered Josh.

Nobody answered. As suddenly as it had started, the

attack had apparently ceased. On the screen the group of adults outside remained immobile. But then a familiar figure pushed her way through to the front.

It was Ms Gresham.

'Children?' she said. 'Can you hear me, children?'

They all looked at each other.

'I know you're listening,' said Ms Gresham. 'Open this door.'

Jasmine watched her. On the monitor, viewed from the ceiling camera, the creature on the back of Ms Gresham's neck looked like a shadow. The back of Jasmine's own neck prickled as she looked from the screen to the pale, panicked faces of the rest of the group.

'You don't understand what's happening here,' said Ms Gresham, her voice sounding perfectly normal. 'That's all it is: a misunderstanding. We can sort everything out, get everyone taken care of. But you have to open this door.'

'What are we going to do?' Lauren murmured.

'Nothing,' Ben hissed. 'You saw her in the lift. We can't trust her.'

'But,' said Lauren, 'she's our teacher.'

Jasmine's mouth was dry.

'Jasmine?' said Ms Gresham, startling her. 'You're more sensible than the others. Listen to me. Tell everyone to stop this foolishness and open this door right now. I'm waiting.'

Ben looked at Jasmine and shook his head.

Jasmine gave him a nod back. Her being 'sensible' was precisely why there was no way she would do what Ms Gresham said – not any more.

But she was thinking: Ms Gresham might be talking, but the way the other adults were still just standing out there had reminded Jasmine of something. It took her a whole, slow second to work out what, but then she got it: *the Barbican staff.*

The people standing outside weren't trying to get in any more; they were *blocking the way out.*

On the screen, Ms Gresham sighed and crossed her arms. 'You're all being very silly,' she said. 'It hurts for a moment, it's true. But then . . . *she* makes everything better.' She paused then added: 'You'll find out.'

Jasmine's gaze snapped upward to the room's ceiling.

Ben looked up too. The ceiling was bare – just white plastic ceiling panels and strip lights. But—

'There!' said Jasmine.

'What?' said Samantha.

'On the wall there! The air-vent! I think it's—!'

'Oh crap!' said Ben.

On the wall above the sink and worktop, the flimsy aluminium slats that led to the air-con ducts were moving. They were being bent and prodded and pushed aside by a number of powerful rubbery legs. The screws that held the duct cover to the wall suddenly came free. The whole thing popped off, dropping into the sink below with a clank.

The first spider-creature dropped in after it. Followed by another, then another.

Screams. Shouting. Chaos. Lauren was up on her chair, shrieking. Josh stood rooted to the spot. Robert shot to his feet and promptly crashed into Hugo, entangling him by the barricade. Jasmine watched helplessly as a creature climbed up the inside of the sink – and launched itself off onto the floor.

'Stop them!' she shouted – narrowly avoiding catching Hugo's flailing elbow in her eye. 'Block the hole, someone, before more of them get in!'

On the wall beside where Ben happened to be standing he'd spotted something: a single board made of cork with a wooden frame, perhaps eighty centimetres wide by forty tall. It was dotted with notices that had been pinned to the cork – details of shifts for the staff, a laminated list of fire-drill procedures and a handwritten sign saying: WASH UP YOUR MUGS!

Ben pulled it off the wall. His first step took him up onto the seat of the chair nearest the sink. His second launched him upwards to land with his feet in the sink itself, crushing one of the creatures that had landed there under the thick soles of his school shoes – but Ben wasn't even looking at it. He was looking at the air-duct's thirty-centimetre-wide hole and the wriggling things about to pour out of it.

Ben slapped the wide notice board over the hole. He felt a sudden and shocking pain in the fingers of both his hands – in the rush of the moment he'd forgotten to make sure they were free of the edges of the board. Pulling his bruised fingers out, he turned and put his back against the board to keep it where it was.

Then he saw what was going on in the room. He was standing in the sink, so he had a pretty good view.

As well as the spider-thing he'd crushed, another already lay flattened and immobile in the centre of the floor. Ben's eyes travelled from the foot that still stood on it, up the leg, and found to his surprise that the person who'd stomped on it was Robert. Robert's eyes, still red from crying, were alight with a savage triumph Ben had never seen in him before.

'There!' screeched Lauren, pointing with a trembling hand at the third creature as it scuttled out from beneath a chair. 'Oh, God! Kill it! *Kill it!*'

Samantha's foot came down: *scrutch*. Splayed out around her shoe, the thing's pale legs gave a convulsive shudder, then went still.

'Are there any others?' asked Jasmine. Her eyes – like those of the rest of the group – were searching every millimetre of the floor.

'Not any more,' said Samantha. She lifted her shoe and gave it a dainty wipe on the carpet.

'Um . . . help?' said Ben. 'A little help over here, please?'

His moment of quick-thinking heroism had passed. He did not like standing in the sink on the squashed remains of a spider-thing while more of them eagerly burrowed and scrabbled at the thin layer of wood between them and his back. He could feel them behind him, the surprising strength of them, pushing and digging. The aluminium duct cover had been no match for them: it could only be moments now before they'd come through the notice board – and then through him.

'The board's not strong enough!' he said. 'I can't hold them!'

Jasmine looked at him. 'Help him, someone!'

Hugo scanned the room. 'Here.' Spotting a metal wastepaper bin in the corner, he grabbed it and tipped out its contents. 'This should keep them out for a bit, at least.'

'Good thinking, mate,' said Josh – while (Ben noticed) taking a cautious step back.

Hugo came on regardless. Ben looked down at him, surprised again. Until this moment he'd always thought of Hugo as just some kind of farting buffoon. But here he was, coming to Ben's rescue without question.

'You think that bin will do the trick?' Ben asked him.

'Get the board out of the way,' said Hugo. 'I'll put this over the hole. Nothing to it.'

'OK then,' said Ben gratefully. 'On three. But I warn you, these things really, *really* want to come in. Ready?'

Hugo nodded.

'One, two . . . *three.*'

Lifting the board clear, Ben jumped past Hugo, landing on a clear spot on the floor and turning quickly. There was a *clank* as Hugo clapped the bin over the hole, then a moment of expectant silence.

Everyone in the room was focused on Hugo. He stood there, his back to the room. But then, still holding the bin in place, he turned and frowned at Ben.

'What?' Ben asked.

In answer, Hugo took the bin off the wall.

No spider-things came out of the hole. The vent was empty.

The creatures had gone.

8:47 PM.

'There,' said Josh, standing back from the bulging clump of maroon and charcoal-grey material he'd been wedging in the hole as best he could. 'That looks solid enough.'

'If those things want to come in again,' said Samantha, 'it's going to take more than our blazers to stop them, don't you think?'

'I told you,' said Josh, 'it's temporary. Just to give us a bit of warning so we can do something else.'

'But *what* else?' asked Samantha. 'What do you think we're going to do? I mean, do you even *know*?'

Josh pursed his lips.

Ben was still feeling slightly humiliated after the creatures' sudden disappearance. But seeing how little Josh enjoyed having his leadership questioned cheered him up a bit.

'I'm sorry,' Josh told Samantha, with a tight, fake smile that Ben knew meant he wasn't sorry at all, 'but I thought it was obvious. We'll keep an eye on the hole in case the spiders come back, of course. If necessary, we'll take shifts. But until they attack again, blocking that hole with anything bigger would mean we can't get to the taps and the sink. And if we stay here much longer,' he added, 'we're going to need those.'

'What for, cups of tea?' asked Samantha. 'Oh yeah, I can see that'd be a big help.'

'Tea,' said Josh, eyes narrowing, 'yes. Water too. But also . . . something else.'

'What?' Samantha asked.

By way of a reply, Josh looked away from Samantha. 'Hugo?'

'Yes, mate?'

'Are you still watching the screens? Are those people still outside the door?'

'No change, mate,' Hugo called back. 'That teacher's gone, but the rest of them are still out there, just . . . standing there. Like they're waiting for something.'

'Waiting for *us*,' said Josh, looking back at Samantha. 'They're on guard, in case we try to come out of these rooms.'

'Yeah,' said Samantha. 'Maybe. So?'

'So,' Jasmine answered for him grimly, from her place on the floor, 'do you notice a *toilet* in here?'

There was a moment of scandalized silence as the full implications hit home.

'No *way*,' Samantha announced. 'There is *no way* I'm going to go to the loo in that sink. Not with you lot right there.'

'Then I hope you don't mind holding it in,' said Josh. 'We could be here a long time.'

Samantha made a contemptuous sucking sound with her teeth, and turned to Jasmine. 'All right then, genius,' she said, changing the subject. 'What about you? Discovered anything yet?'

'I'm . . . not sure,' said Jasmine.

She had retrieved the flattened remains of the three dead creatures and was now using the notice board on her lap as

CRAWLERS

a makeshift dissecting table. Well, strictly speaking she was poking at them with a biro, but that was the best she could do in the circumstances. English might be Jasmine's weakest subject but biology, supposedly, was her strongest. Examining the creatures seemed a sensible next step: it might give her an idea of what they were up against. But so far all that she had managed to do was disgust herself.

Each spider-thing was about twenty centimetres across. Instead of eight legs though, weirdly, they had five – four long ones on one side of their wide, flattened bodies and only one, a thicker one, on the other. Also, apart from a thin band of red at the joints of each of their legs, they were almost transparent – like jellyfish. The creatures were nearly as unpleasant dead as they had been alive. They gave off a faint fishy smell and they were sticky to the touch. There was something deeply wrong about their see-through legs and the little strips of blood at their joints. Jasmine was not squeamish, but the rubbery way the creatures' flesh resisted the push of her pen made her gorge rise.

None of this was visible to anyone else. To Ben, Jasmine seemed as unfazed as if she dissected monsters every day of the week.

'What have you found?' he asked, even more impressed by Jasmine than he had been before. 'What are these things? Where do they come from?'

'I honestly don't know,' she admitted. 'These animals . . . they're not like anything I've ever seen before.'

Ben looked at her. 'What makes you say that?' he asked.

'Well, for one thing' – Jasmine grimaced – 'it looks like they don't have any . . . *orifices.*'

Samantha made a snorting sound in her nose. Lauren sniggered. Jasmine sighed.

'Er, what about the mouth, though?' asked Ben. 'We've seen them bite, so . . .'

'That's just it,' said Jasmine, pointing. 'Look: they've all got these two probosces . . .'

'Pro-*whatties*?' said Samantha.

'Like needles,' Jasmine explained. 'A pair of them, very sharp, for puncturing skin. But that's it. There's nothing here you could really call a mouth, and nowhere I can see for food to go. In fact . . .' She paused. 'I think that whatever this creature is doing when it bites, it's got nothing to do with eating at all.'

'What do you think it's doing, then?' asked Josh, without much patience.

Jasmine looked at him. 'I've . . . got a theory,' she said carefully.

'When Ms Gresham got bit,' put in Samantha, 'she just seemed to go mental – right?'

'Her eyes were weird,' said Ben.

'It was the same with the Barbican staff,' Jasmine told him, glad he'd noticed that. 'When we were trying to get them to let us out, they had the same look.'

'And then the people outside,' said Ben. 'The way they attacked, the way they stopped – it was all at once. Almost like . . .'

'Like they're being *controlled*,' said Jasmine.

Ben and Jasmine looked at each other.

'So you're saying . . .' Josh began. 'Wait, what are you saying? That what we've got here is some kind of spider that *takes over your mind*?'

'Like I said,' said Jasmine, looking down, 'it's just a theory. Anyway,' she added a little defensively, 'I don't think you could really say they're spiders.'

'We could call them something else,' said Ben, eager to help. 'How about . . . crawlers?'

'Excuse me,' said Samantha, putting up a hand. 'Hello?'

Everyone turned to look at her.

'This conversation is fascinating to you, maybe,' she said, 'but we've got a bit of a situation here, don't you think? For a start, I mean, is *anyone's* phone working yet? Anybody?'

Lauren flipped her mobile open, then shut it again glumly.

'Well there you go,' said Samantha. 'No phone. No Internet. Not even texts – and believe me, I've tried.'

'What's your point?' asked Jasmine.

'If we'd kept moving,' said Samantha, 'we might have been all right, but oh no! Thanks to you we're stuck here, with no phones, no food, and not even a *toilet*. What I want to know is, what are we going to do about it?'

'I don't know – Samantha, wasn't it?' said Josh with icy politeness. 'If you have any thoughts to share I'd be delighted to hear them. What do *you* suggest we "do about it"?'

'You're the one who put himself in charge,' Samantha snapped back. 'What made you feel you could do that, by the way? What makes you the boss here? Have you got some special qualifications we should know about, or what?'

'You mean, do I have any prior experience of being attacked by' – Josh sneered at Ben and made quote marks in the air – '"*crawlers*", then trapped in a room?' He smiled at Samantha mirthlessly. 'I'm afraid not.'

'Then what gives you the right to put all our lives in danger like this?'

Josh's smile froze.

'Samantha . . .' said Jasmine warningly.

'No, you just shut it too, *Jasmine*,' said Samantha, not even looking at her. 'I mean listen to you, all of you, poncing along with your "I've got a theory". What are we doing here? Why is this happening to us? What's going on? *When are we going to get out?*'

'For God's sake,' roared Josh, 'that's precisely what we're trying to *work out*, you stupid pleb!'

Ben blinked, and there was a sharp intake of breath from the rest of the group. Here it was: the side to Josh he'd always suspected, the side that people at Walsingham pretended wasn't there.

The effect was immediate.

'Why, you stuck-up . . .' began Samantha.

'. . . snot-nosed . . .' said Lauren.

'. . . arrogant little public-school *git*!' Samantha finished. 'How *dare* you call me a pleb?' Apart from two hard spots of red on either side of her nose, her face had gone pale with rage. 'But that's what you think of us,' she added, triumphant now, hitting her stride. 'That's what you *all* think of us, all of you, isn't it?' she repeated, turning to include all the boys.

Uh-oh . . . thought Ben.

'Just 'cause your parents paid money to send you to school, you think that gives you the right to look down on the rest of the world. Look at yourselves,' said Samantha, 'acting the boss, giving orders like you're born to rule.'

'Oh, for God's sake,' Josh repeated, rolling his eyes. 'For your information, the only reason I took charge is because nobody else did!'

Samantha snorted. 'Yeah, right.'

'It's true! I didn't hear *you* coming up with any ideas until we were in here. Come to that, you haven't said anything worth a damn *since*, either. All you do is bitch about how your mobile doesn't work!'

'Don't call her a bitch!' put in Lauren.

'What?' Josh blinked. 'I didn't! I said "bitch", as in "to bitch", verb, meaning "complain and whine and drone on about everything". What are you, stupid?'

'Stop calling us stupid!' shrieked Samantha.

'Shut up a second, all of you!' yelled Jasmine. 'You,' she added, pointing at Hugo, who was standing in the doorway, looking startled in the sudden silence. 'What is it now?'

'It's . . . one of the screens,' stammered Hugo, bewildered. 'The camera that covers the main entrance to the street. Some police are trying to get in!'

'Well, about bloody time.' Samantha sniffed. 'Out of my way, I want to see what's going on.'

Elbowing Josh aside, she strode past him and Hugo. Josh turned, as if about to say something, but his way was blocked by Lauren, who now stood between him and the monitor-room door, arms crossed, face set, like a sneering female bouncer.

'For God's sake,' said Josh, a third time.

But Jasmine had dodged behind him too. Now she, Hugo and Samantha were all in front of the monitors.

The first thing Jasmine noticed was that most of the screens were empty. Or rather, they continued to show the parts of the

Barbican covered by their cameras. But apart from the eerily silent adults outside their own door, no other people could be seen except on the monitor Hugo was indicating.

'But . . . there's only two of them!' said Samantha after a moment, annoyed.

It was true. The view of the Barbican's main glass entrance doors was grainy, bluish, a little unfocused, but the two police officers currently trying to get in appeared clearly enough: one man, one woman, dressed in regular uniform – ordinary street police.

'Why's there only two?' said Samantha.

'Because they don't know what's happening,' said Jasmine, realizing. 'They probably only came because someone heard the alarm. You said yourself: mobiles don't work here. And for all we know, we could be the only people in the building who haven't been bitten. Maybe no one outside has any idea what's really going on.'

'But it must seem a bit weird that the doors are locked . . . right?' asked Hugo. Then: 'Look, one of them's going for his radio.'

While the female officer looked for a doorbell or buzzer, the male one lifted his lapel radio to his lips. But Jasmine knew he would only be saying something like 'We're checking it out.'

Suddenly there was movement on another of the monitors. Six Barbican staff – two men and four women – were now walking up the wide white passage that led to the entrance.

'Where did they come from?' asked Samantha, pointing.

'Shhhhh,' said Jasmine. 'Watch.'

Onscreen, the six staff members approached the glass doors. While one, a woman in a smart knee-length skirt and fitted jacket, made 'just a moment' gestures, the others set to work, reaching up and down, busying themselves with the locks at the tops and bottoms of the heavy glass panels. Finally one of them held the door open, and the smart lady beckoned the two police officers inside.

'Oh no . . .' said Jasmine.

The next bit happened very fast. As soon as the two officers were inside, the rest of the welcoming committee dropped their pretence with the locks. Two of them produced what they'd been hiding behind their backs and – as the others blocked the door – strode up to the unsuspecting officers while they were talking to the smart lady. They didn't stand a chance: before they could even react it was over. The two police went rigid then fell to the floor, with crawlers on the backs of their necks.

9:08 PM.

'What?' asked Josh as Samantha and Jasmine came out of the monitor room. 'What happened?'

'I . . . don't know,' said Samantha. Her voice sounded small and strange after all her bluster from before. 'There were two police officers. Some people let them in, and . . .' She paused and looked wildly at Jasmine. 'That can't be all, right? Those can't be the only ones coming to help us. Everybody knows we're stuck in here! Any second now they're going to come and . . . and . . .'

Lauren looked uncertain for a moment, then her arm went around Samantha's shoulders. She took her over to a chair and sat her down.

Everyone else looked at Jasmine.

She took another deep breath. 'All right, everybody,' she said, 'I'm going to tell you something. You're not going to like it, so I'll tell it to you straight: I don't think anyone's coming to help us. For now, we're on our own.'

There was a moment of silence, then a rising hubbub of voices.

'What do you mean?'

'Of course they're coming to help us – why wouldn't they?'

'When are we going to get out of here?'

Jasmine waited for a chance to continue. She didn't get it. Until—

'*Quiet!*' roared Hugo from behind her. *Then* there was silence.

'Er, thank you,' said Jasmine.

Hugo, who was standing in the doorway, didn't acknowledge the thanks; he looked at Jasmine, just like everyone else was doing – again. She had to swallow before starting to explain.

'The two police who came to the door . . .' she began. 'Well, I think they just happened to be passing by. They had no idea. The fact is, right now I don't think anyone outside knows that any of this is going on.'

'But . . . we'll be missed,' said Josh.

'So will all those other people,' said Robert.

'Not for a while yet, though,' Ben put in bleakly. 'We're all supposed to be at the theatre, remember? The play wasn't even due to finish till after ten.'

'After that, though,' said Jasmine, wanting to soften the blow, keep people's spirits up, 'you're right: people are going to wonder where we are. Calls will get made. Someone will come and investigate. You obviously can't keep something like this a secret for ever. Besides, the police radioed in to say they were checking the doors. But' – she hesitated – 'that was before they . . .'

'Before they what?' asked Ben.

'The crawlers got them,' said Samantha dully.

'*What?*' said Lauren.

'It's true,' said Jasmine. 'Some Barbican staff, ones who'd

been bitten, tricked them into coming in. Then, while their backs were turned, they—'

'Oh God!' said Lauren, taking her arm off Samantha's shoulder. 'But if they got the *police*, then what chance have we got?' She blinked, and her bottom lip started to wobble again. 'We're – we're going to *die* in here, aren't we?'

'Now, come on!' said Jasmine, with a firmness she didn't feel. The situation and what she'd seen were taking their toll on her too, and she was wondering how long her outward cool was going to hold. But she forced herself. 'Come *on*,' she repeated. 'It's all going to be all right.' Remembering that the last person who'd said this was Ms Gresham, she added: 'Listen to what I'm telling you. Help will come at some point, definitely. We've . . .' She shrugged helplessly. 'We've just got to sit tight and wait.'

'But . . . what about the ones who've been bitten?' asked Hugo. 'The way those things attach themselves to you looks pretty nasty.'

'Hugo . . .' said Josh.

'No,' said Hugo, oblivious to how little he was helping. 'No, listen: what if, when you get one of those things on you, you *die*? When you walk around afterwards maybe you *are* some kind of zombie, like the films. Maybe the spider-things *eat your brain* and – yeah! – maybe the only bits of your mind that they leave behind are the bits that help you find *more people*, with more brains to eat. And—'

'Hugo!' said Josh.

'Yes, mate?'

Josh just looked at him.

'Oh,' said Hugo, going red. 'Um. Sorry. I'll just, ah, watch the monitors.' He stepped through the doorway again, closing the door behind him.

There was a long silence.

'Well,' said Josh, with obvious effort, 'the barricade with the lockers looks pretty secure, at least. And I blocked the air-vent myself. We'll be watching it: the . . . crawlers' – he grimaced – 'won't be able to get in, not that way, not without us noticing.' He clapped his hands loudly and gave a horribly enthusiastic grin. 'So! Since we've got some time on our hands, why don't we all have a bit of a sing-song? Come on now: who knows a good one to start with?'

Everyone stared at him.

'I'm joking,' he said.

Nobody laughed.

9:21 PM.

'My Queen?' said Steadman, interrupting again. 'One of our police stations has noticed that those two officers aren't responding to radio.'

He paused as if this news was significant.

'Well?' he asked, when I didn't reply. 'Aren't you going to do something?'

'What do you suggest I do, Steadman?' I asked back, through the young man's mouth.

'The *obvious* step, one would think, would be for you to *make* those two police call in. Use your power on them. Do what you do. If you don't, very soon you're going to have a lot more of them on your hands.'

'That,' I told him, 'is precisely my intention.'

The speakers on the pit's brick walls were silent again for a moment.

'You *want* more people to come?' said Steadman. 'Are you sure you can handle that?'

'You doubt me?'

'Not at all,' Steadman blustered. 'It's just that—'

'It's just that in your experiments on me down here,' I told him, 'I ruled just a few at a time. You weren't alive to witness my power all those years ago; you've never seen for yourself the full extent of what I can do. So now I rule some two thousand subjects in this building of yours, you worry I'm not really strong enough to rule more. Correct?'

'Tell me again how it works,' said Steadman.

The voice from the speakers was thick, urgent, with none of the arrogance to which I had grown all too accustomed.

Steadman needed reassurance: to continue to believe in me he required another glimpse of what I was offering him. So, for what I hoped was the last time, I gave him a reply.

'When you feel my hand upon you, Steadman,' I began, 'you experience two things. The first is the physical shock as I penetrate your nervous system, but that is brief; next comes what will feel like complete and total *normality*. You simply find that all your wishes now coincide with mine. They will coincide so sweetly,' I told him, 'that you might not even be aware of a difference.'

'Less of the "you", please,' growled the voice from the speakers. 'I'm not one of your subjects and I'm not going to be. May I remind you that we are in this as equals: you need me, *my Queen*, and don't you forget it.'

'A slip of the tongue,' I assured him. 'Please let me continue.'

'Very well.'

'I can control my subjects directly if I choose, of course. But the simplest and most efficient way to rule is to allow them to *rule themselves* – to let their own natures limit and shape them to my purpose.'

'And what exactly do you mean by that?'

'When my hand is upon someone I know everything about them. I see what they see. I experience the world as they do. But I also know the contents of their minds

– the deepest secrets of their lives. One of those secrets is this: the vast majority *want* to be ruled. They may pretend independence but in fact they crave acceptance, approval, the comfort of the herd. They want their decisions made for them. They long to be directed by a higher power . . .' I paused. 'By us.'

'You are . . . persuasive, my Queen,' said Steadman. 'But I'd be more confident you can keep your end of our bargain if those *schoolchildren* weren't still on the loose.'

'I told you, Steadman,' I said patiently. 'They didn't escape – and I can prove it. Would you like to hear a secret from one of the youngsters right now?'

'You can do that?' said Steadman.

Concentrating, I picked one.

'It is a memory of school,' I told him. 'All tonight's adult subjects, too, have strong school memories: those years seem strangely significant to your kind. But this memory is particularly potent, being *recent*.

'It concerns a note passed during a lesson. The note is folded many times; its paper is soft and faintly greasy from the touch of many fingers. I unfold it carefully and find that the note has been signed, not just by one person, but by the whole class: twenty-two of my peers have put their name to what it says. When I read the message, my skin goes hot and tight and I tingle all over.'

I paused, intrigued. The memory was harsh and bitter. I felt the squirming sensation in my subject's guts. I noticed how, in the memory, the background sounds of the class and the other details of the moment seemed to fade and shrink, until four words were all that was left.

'Well?' asked Steadman. 'What does it say?'

'The signed note says,' I told Steadman, '*We all hate you.*'

For a moment Steadman was silent. 'Kids,' he said – but the amusement in his voice was false. I suspected that he had similar secrets from his own school years. I looked forward to discovering them.

'Am I to understand, then,' he asked quickly, 'that someone in that room is already under your control?'

'Correct. I have already begun to undermine the most effective members of the group, and the others got this far only by luck. These children are no threat. Soon, if I keep them where they are, they will neutralize themselves.'

'So,' I told him, 'send more adults for me to rule.'

9:34 PM.

'This is ridiculous,' said Ben, getting up. 'We can't just sit here. There's got to be something we can do. Something else we can figure out about this situation – or some way to get word to the outside.'

'Like I said before, mate,' said Josh, looking at his fingernails, 'I'm open to suggestions. If you've got something to say I'm sure we'd all be happy to hear it. But if you don't, I'd just as soon you sit down and keep quiet, if you don't mind.' He smiled – or at least, the corners of his mouth lifted: the smile didn't reach his eyes. 'Help will be here soon enough. No sense rocking the boat.'

'I want to have a look at those monitors,' said Ben, advancing towards the door.

'Be my guest,' said Josh. 'I'm sure Hugo could use a break, anyhow.'

'Why, *thank you*, Josh,' said Ben, but he didn't wait to see if Josh caught the sarcasm. 'Hugo,' he said, closing the door to the monitor room behind him, 'what's going on?'

Hugo looked up from the screens and blinked. 'What? Oh . . . nothing.' He gestured. 'See for yourself.'

On all the screens except one, the scenes the cameras were looking at were empty: empty passageways; empty stairwells; empty rooms – no people at all. But on the screen showing the view in the passage outside . . .

This was the first time Ben had seen what was waiting for them, guarding their only exit. These had been ordinary adults on a night out: they were now standing absolutely still, like mannequins.

'How many of them are out there?' he asked, stifling a shudder.

'Twenty-seven of them that you can see there,' said Hugo. 'There are probably more behind, but I counted all the ones I could. Three times, actually.'

'Not much else to do in here, huh?' said Ben.

'You're not wrong,' said Hugo drily.

'That's not all of them out there, though, is it?' asked Ben.

'How d'you mean?'

'You think all of the bitten people are out there in the passageway? What about the ones who went out to meet the police? Were they from out there?'

'Not that I saw,' Hugo answered. 'If they did come from the crowd outside, it wasn't from the front row. No one's twitched a muscle in that lot since they stopped trying to break the door down.' He made a face. 'It's freaking me out, frankly.'

'So maybe,' said Ben, 'not everybody who's been bitten is there.'

Hugo shrugged. 'Stands to reason, I guess.'

'Well, if they're not out there,' Ben wondered, looking at the empty screens, 'where *are* they all?'

'Beats me,' said Hugo. 'I just work here.'

Ben looked down at the desk at which Hugo was sitting. As well as the congealed remains of a mug of milky coffee and an impressive (and obviously long-lived) collection of empty sweet wrappers left by its usual occupants, the desk contained a black angled console covered in numbered, grey rubber buttons with, at its centre, a small joystick.

'This looks like it controls the cameras,' said Ben, reaching for the buttons. 'Why don't we take a look?'

'Now hold on a second,' said Hugo, turning on his chair and putting himself in between Ben and the console. 'I don't think that's a good idea.'

'What? Why not?'

Hugo pursed his lips. Ben could tell that he didn't like being put in the position of having to stop him – but Ben didn't care.

'Come on, Hugo,' he said. 'What's the problem?'

'All right,' said Hugo, 'I'll tell you: right now, we've got a good combination. There' – he pointed – 'are the two screens showing the main entrance, and we've got this camera showing us what's happening out there in the passage. If we start pressing buttons, we might lose that picture. Then we'd have no idea what they're up to. We'd be defenceless.'

'Cobblers,' said Ben. 'I'm sure it's not complicated. If that happens we just keep pressing the buttons until the picture comes back.'

'But what if they attack again while we can't see them?'

'They won't! They've been standing out there doing nothing for, like, an hour. Besides, what difference would it make? They'd still be out there and we'd still be stuck in here.' Ben tried to reach past him, but—

'No, I'm sorry.' Hugo shook his head. 'There's no way I'm letting you do it. It's too risky.'

'But . . .' Ben stared at him, amazed. 'Isn't it sort of worth the risk? I mean . . . those screens are the only advantage we've got. Apart from a couple of squashed crawlers, they're the only thing that might give us an idea of what's really going on in this place. And you're seriously telling me you won't even take a look?'

Hugo blinked rapidly. 'What did you call them?' Then he collected himself. 'I mean, *no*. No changing the cameras. Or not without Josh's say-so anyhow.' He folded his arms, doing his best to look decisive.

'You're kidding,' said Ben. 'You need Josh's permission? You won't even press a button without Josh holding your hand?'

'It's not that,' Hugo blustered. 'I just don't think it's a good idea, that's all.'

Ben was going to say exactly what he thought about that, but was interrupted.

'What's going on?' Josh asked, closing the door behind him.

'Ben wants to change what's on the monitors,' said Hugo promptly.

'Why?' asked Josh. 'You can't get the Sci-Fi channel on

here, you know.' He smirked at Hugo. 'I mean, honestly, Ben: *crawlers?*' Josh shook his head in mock despair, then gave Ben another smile – a smile that was no smile at all.

'We should try and see what else is going on in the rest of the building,' said Ben, keeping his voice level. How he hated having to explain himself! Especially to Josh. And he might not even have had to, if Hugo'd had the gumption to think for himself. 'We might get some clues about what to do.'

Josh sighed. 'But we know what to do, don't we? We're going to wait here until help comes. We decided.'

'*I* didn't decide,' said Ben.

Josh narrowed his eyes. 'Excuse me?'

'I said, I didn't decide. I don't remember it being put to a vote or anything. In fact,' Ben added, 'nobody's really asked anybody's opinion at all – and certainly not mine. But it seems to me that somehow we've ended up doing whatever *you* tell us to do, Josh. Why is that, exactly?'

'What's the matter, Ben?' asked Josh softly. 'You don't like the way I run things?'

Surprised, Ben didn't reply.

'That's fine,' said Josh. 'Really – it's fine. In school circumstances, I'd be happy to listen to any problems you might have. You know I'd always have time for you, mate.'

'But—' said Ben.

'But this isn't school circumstances, is it?' asked Josh, interrupting him again. 'This is something else. Something bad. Something,' he added, 'for which we all have to pull together.'

'What?'

'You know what I'm talking about,' said Josh, leaning back against the door to make sure it was closed behind him. 'Don't pretend you don't. I'm talking about those plebs out there.'

There it was again. That word.

'Someone has to get them through this.' Josh spoke low and quickly now. 'Someone has to *lead them*. They'll bitch and moan, of course. But they *want* to be told what to do. They're plebs. They're happiest that way. One thing, though: there can't be more than one leader.' He paused. 'You see, it's like the army.'

Hugo nodded vigorously.

'There has to be a clear chain of command,' said Josh. 'One person has authority in a crisis situation: the buck stops with them, their word goes. That's how it should be. It can't be any other way. Because in a crisis situation if there's any hesitation, any questioning orders, people die.

'Here's the thing, mate: this group needs a leader. No offence, but I don't think you or anyone else out there is up to the job. So it's time for you to make a choice. You can carry on like you always do – keeping yourself apart, sneering at us all from the sidelines. Or you can do the right thing for once, stand shoulder to shoulder with the rest of us, and *back me up a little*.' Josh smiled. 'That's all I'm asking.'

Ben frowned. 'And all *I'm* asking,' he said, 'is to have a go on the cameras. Why are you being such a knob about this?'

Josh's smile vanished. His lips tightened into a hard white line. 'All right,' he told Ben slowly. 'I've given you your warning. Now all bets are off. From now on, I'm *watching you*.'

'Really,' said Ben.

'You're a bad apple, Freeman,' said Josh. 'By crossing me, you put the whole group in danger. So, cross me again? You'll be history.'

'Let me get this straight,' said Ben. 'You're *not* going to let me use the cameras?'

'Get out of here,' said Josh. 'Before I lose my temper.'

'Oh, we wouldn't want that,' said Ben, pushing past him. 'Knob.'

9:39 PM.

Ben emerged from the monitor room with his face feeling hot and red. He was annoyed with Josh, sure, but he was also annoyed at himself. Why couldn't he keep his cool with him? Whenever Ben spoke to Josh he got a twisting feeling in his stomach and then all of a sudden the conversation would be out of control. He hadn't meant to call Josh a knob. Well all right, he *had* meant to – Josh unquestionably was one, after all. But the sensible thing in the circumstances would've been to try reasoning with him some more, before reaching for the insults.

Yeah, he told himself bitterly, *like that would've worked*.

They just hated each other. That was all there was to it. Or rather, he hated Josh; most of the time Josh probably didn't even think about him. Josh was too busy being top of the school heap, giving orders and having everybody do as he said.

He looked up. Despite being stuck together for the best part of two hours now, the group had spectacularly failed to mix. Robert and Ben himself were on the side of the room nearest the monitor-room door. The girls – Jasmine, Samantha, Lauren and the mousey-haired one, Ben couldn't think of her name for a moment . . . *Lisa* – were all sitting on chairs or the floor on the opposite side of the room. The room was divided down the middle, by both school and gender.

Deliberately not pausing to think about it too much – but feeling a flare of nerves anyway – Ben walked over and sat down on the floor next to Jasmine.

'Hi,' he said.

Jasmine stopped prodding at the dead crawlers. Setting the notice board and its grisly contents down beside her, she looked at him.

'Anything happening on the screens?' she asked, all business.

'Er . . . no,' said Ben, surprised.

He thought of saying something about the argument with Josh and Hugo, but hesitated: he might have sounded like he was telling tales, and – annoyingly – there was something of Josh's words about 'pulling together' in his thoughts too. Ben felt powerfully attracted to Jasmine: she seemed the only other person in this mad situation who was making any effort to find out what was really happening and, yes, she was gorgeous. But he wasn't quite ready to say what he thought of Josh just yet. Also, by the time he realized that this was what he was feeling, the moment had gone.

'Oh well,' said Jasmine. 'Then I guess we really do just have to sit and wait.'

'I'm Ben,' Ben blurted.

Jasmine gave him a quizzical look. 'Yes,' she said. 'I know.'

'You're Jasmine – right?' said Ben. But Jasmine's expression did not change. In fact, from the silence of the room around him Ben imagined that everybody else was looking at him now too. He hoped his face wasn't still red, but he reckoned it probably was.

'It's just . . . nobody's talking,' he plunged on when Jasmine didn't answer. *Brilliant*, he thought. *What's that, three obvious things in a row?* 'We're all just sitting here.' *Four.* 'We don't know how long for.' *Five.* 'So I thought, er, maybe we should try and get to know each other a bit.' *Oh, great, now it probably sounds like I'm trying to chat her up!* 'Just to pass the time, yeah?' he added quickly. 'So, you know' – he shrugged – 'hi.'

'Hi yourself,' said Jasmine.

It was probably only because she thought Ben was a fool – how could she think otherwise, after the lamest introduction in world history? – but at least now she was smiling. She had a tiny dimple in her left cheek, and the tip of her nose had lifted a little: Jasmine's whole face moved when she smiled.

She has a nice smile, Ben decided.

'Kind of a weird way to meet,' he tried, brilliantly.

'Yes, you could say that,' was the judicious reply.

'I mean, I don't think anything like this has ever happened to me before,' said Ben, grinning himself now. 'You?'

If Jasmine had a type of boy she liked – and she wasn't sure she did – Ben shouldn't have been it. He was white, for a start. That by itself wasn't necessarily a problem, but Jasmine had never thought about a white person in a romantic way before. Especially one with freckles, and floppy dark hair, and sparkling grey-blue eyes, and a cute grin, and—

Now hold on a second. She blinked.

'No,' she said aloud, 'I think I can safely say that nothing like this has ever happened to me, either.'

'When we get out of this,' said Ben, trying to make light of it, 'we can sell this story to the papers. We'll make a fortune.'

'Yes – when we get out of this,' Jasmine echoed.

'What's up?' Ben asked quietly.

Jasmine cast a quick glance at the three dead crawlers, which were still lying on the notice board on the floor beside her, their rubbery legs in the air. Then she looked at him.

'Did you see the monitors?' she asked. 'The people outside?'

'Yes . . .' said Ben, the intense way she'd asked the question making him feel uncertain.

'What do they look like they're doing?'

'Nothing,' said Ben. 'Standing there, I guess. Waiting. Guarding, like Josh said.'

'But *why*? Why did they stop attacking? And why did the crawlers go away?'

'What do you mean?'

'You said you saw thousands of them,' Jasmine reminded him, 'before, in the foyer.'

'Yes,' said Ben, 'but—'

'Then there should have been more in the vent when they attacked us. A notice board wouldn't have stopped them. The room should have been full of them. But instead . . .' She paused. 'Instead, they just *left*. And we're being kept here. What I want to know is, why?'

'For Christ's sake,' said Samantha loudly from behind them, 'what difference does it make? We're stuck here!'

'Yeah,' chipped in Lauren immediately, 'why've you got to keep banging on about it?'

Jasmine rolled her eyes.

Ben was just about to try changing the subject, when:

'Hey,' said Jasmine, standing up suddenly. 'Hey. Hey! *Hey!*'

'What?' said Ben.

'Oh!' said Jasmine, making a face. 'Oh, that's *really* funny, I don't think. All right, who did it? Who? Own up now, or I'm going to get angry.'

'What? What are you on about *now*?' asked Samantha.

'You!' Jasmine snapped back, rounding on her. 'Don't pretend! This is something you and Lauren cooked up, isn't it? Some *stupid* little game of yours. Well I'm telling you, it isn't funny.'

'*Don't*,' said Samantha, getting to her feet, 'call me stupid.'

'Uh, Jasmine?' asked Ben. 'What exactly is the problem?'

'Can't you see?' Jasmine pointed at her improvised dissection table. The notice board still lay on the floor, where she'd put it. But: 'One of the crawlers has *gone*!'

9:48 PM.

For a moment there was silence in the room. It was true. Of the three squashed crawlers that Jasmine had been examining, now only two remained.

'But . . . where is it?' asked Robert, in a voice that was dangerously quiet.

Ben noticed that Lisa too had suddenly drawn both her legs up off the floor, and had wrapped her arms around them, hugging herself.

'It was dead . . .' he said, looking at Jasmine. 'Right?'

'Of course it was dead,' Jasmine snapped. 'I mean,' she added more kindly, 'it was squashed, right? So someone must have taken it. And I bet I know who.'

'Listen,' said Samantha, 'I've been sitting here all the time. So even if I wanted to, which I don't, how could I have taken it without you noticing?'

'You just waited until I wasn't looking. Or if it wasn't *you*, then it was your *lapdog*.'

'What?' said Lauren, realizing everyone's attention was now on her. 'No! What would I want with one of them things?'

'Let me guess,' scoffed Jasmine. 'You're going to dangle it in someone's face, or something equally hilarious.'

'I wouldn't touch them.' Lauren shuddered. 'No way. They're horrible!'

'Look, there were three crawlers before,' said Jasmine. 'Now there are two. Someone in this room must have taken one.'

'Or maybe,' Samantha pointed out, 'it went off by itself.'

There was a pause.

'Well, OK,' said Ben, getting up. 'I guess we'd better search the room. Jasmine, maybe you'd better take the board and go stand over there by the sink. We don't want the other two disappearing. The rest of you' – he shrugged – 'wherever you are now, that's your corner. Search every bit of it as carefully as you can.'

Everyone did as he said, to Ben's surprise. The room wasn't big, and it had six people in it. Ben's spot wasn't much bigger than he was: he felt stupid checking under neighbouring chairs and groping around the carpet with his hands, and he felt sure he wasn't the only one. But at that moment the door to the monitor room opened and Josh emerged. Everyone turned.

Josh looked noticeably paler than before, like he'd just had some kind of shock. He stared blankly at the expectant faces for a moment, then said: 'What are you doing?'

'One of the dead crawlers is missing,' Ben explained dutifully.

'What do you mean, missing?'

'We've just searched the room,' said Ben. He looked around. Everyone shook their heads. 'No sign so far.'

Josh frowned. 'Well it can't have vanished into thin air. What do you think's happened to it?'

'Someone's taken it,' said Jasmine, from her spot by the sink.

'Really?' asked Josh. 'What for?'

'For a joke,' said Jasmine. 'Or—' She stopped.

'Or what?' asked Josh.

'Samantha thought it might have come back to life, or something,' said Ben.

'Good grief,' said Josh. 'Well . . . never mind that for now.'

Ben stared at him.

'I've got news,' he went on. 'Just a few minutes ago two more police cars arrived at the main entrance.'

'All right!' said Lauren. 'We're saved!'

'Erm,' said Josh, 'don't get too excited just yet.'

'Why not?' asked Lauren.

'What happened?' asked Jasmine.

Josh hesitated, then said: 'They . . . didn't *all* get captured this time. That's the main thing. One of the police was wounded—'

'*Wounded?*' Everyone was starting to react now. 'What? How?'

'But he managed to escape!' said Josh, making 'calm down' gestures with his hands. 'He got out before they could reach him, so he didn't get bitten and you can bet he'll be calling for backup *right now*. The secret's out, people,' he added with an enthusiasm that, to Ben, was belied by the sickly look on his face. 'I'm *sure* more police will be along soon, together with the army and . . . and everybody. So until then, all we've got to do is stay here and wait.'

'That's what you said before,' said a voice – Samantha's. When Josh turned and saw the look she was giving him he faltered and, for once, was at a loss for a reply.

Jasmine took a step towards Josh. 'Was it very bad?' she asked quietly.

'It was so . . . quick,' Josh admitted. 'The way the bitten people lured the police in and got them so easily. It . . . did rather take me by surprise. Yes.'

'Do you and Hugo want to take a break from watching the cameras?' Jasmine suggested.

'Thank you,' said Josh. 'But—'

'Ben and I could take a turn,' said Jasmine quickly. 'Couldn't we, Ben?'

'Er . . . sure,' said Ben, surprised. 'I mean, yes, definitely.'

'It's settled then.'

Before Josh could draw breath to protest Jasmine had already passed him and opened the door.

Hugo was sitting hunched in front of the screen. At the sound of the door he sniffed heavily before turning: his eyes were red and his face, like Josh's, was pale. Whatever they'd just seen had obviously hit both boys hard.

'We've come to give you some time off,' said Jasmine, smiling sweetly.

Hugo blinked, dubious. 'OK,' he said finally. He sniffed again and looked hard at Ben. 'But don't *touch* anything.'

When the door had closed behind him, Jasmine sat down on the chair and leaned back. 'Ben,' she said, 'we have to talk.'

10:02 PM.

'What I'm about to tell you,' said Jasmine, 'has got to be a secret. OK? You'll understand why as soon as you hear it, but first I've got to have your promise: this shouldn't be shared with anyone — not even the guys from your school. I . . .' She looked at him. 'I don't know how well you get on with them?'

'Not particularly well,' Ben admitted.

'That's what I figured,' said Jasmine. She gave Ben a quick smile. 'To be honest, I'm kind of the same way.' The smile faded. 'But I'm deadly serious: can you promise you won't tell?'

Ben frowned. 'Um, that kind of depends on what you're going to tell me, doesn't it?'

Jasmine blinked.

'I mean, this is a mad situation we're in,' Ben explained. 'I can't go making promises that might turn out to be dangerous later on down the road, can I?' He tried for a smile.

'Well you're right about one thing,' said Jasmine, not smiling back. 'This situation is definitely mad. But I reckon it might be even worse than you think.' She paused and put her head on one side, giving Ben a critical look.

There was a moment of silence between them.

Ben wanted to say something to make himself sound more impressive. Under Jasmine's gaze he found himself pushing his chest out a little and trying to make his expression as straight as possible.

'OK,' said Jasmine. 'You seem like someone I can trust.'

'You too!' Ben was so pleased, he'd replied without thinking, and now he felt very embarrassed. *What a stupid thing to say*, he told himself.

'I'm worried someone in our group might already have been bitten,' said Jasmine bluntly – bringing Ben back to the present with a bump. She nodded past him at the door and the people beyond it. 'Maybe the person who took the crawler did it because they want to use it on someone else, somehow – put *them* under control too.' She paused. 'I think we might have a traitor in the group.'

'What?' Ben stared at her, gobsmacked. 'But . . . how?'

'It must have happened in the foyer, before we all got

in the lift. Maybe it helps explain why the adults stopped attacking so suddenly: they've got a spy in the room. They're *watching us.*'

'Wait!' said Ben, putting his hands up. 'Hold on a second!'

'What?' asked Jasmine.

Ben looked at her. He was impressed by how cool she was, the way she was analysing their situation in the middle of all this weirdness. He wanted to agree with her, he really did, but . . .

'Everything that's been happening definitely seems to be organized somehow,' he began. 'I'm with you that far, for sure. Those people outside, and the way they stopped attacking when the crawlers were coming through the vent . . .' He pointed at the screen. 'That was *co-ordinated.* That isn't how zombies normally behave – or, um' – he tried for a smile – 'not in the films *I've* seen, anyhow. But what gives you the idea that someone in the group is a traitor?'

To Jasmine, Ben's smile didn't look friendly or self-deprecating. To Jasmine, Ben's smile looked like he was patronizing her.

'Fact one,' she told him, 'one of the crawlers is missing. Agreed?'

'Sure,' said Ben. 'Of course.'

'We searched the room. It's a small room with no way in

or out, and there are plenty of us to do the searching. But – fact two – we didn't find it. Right?'

'Yes,' said Ben, 'that's true, but—'

'It's like Josh said,' Jasmine interrupted (at the mention of the other boy's name Ben's smile fell). 'The crawler couldn't vanish into thin air. So there's only one other possible explanation for why we couldn't find it – right? Someone in the group *didn't want it to be found.*'

'Someone who's already been bitten,' said Ben. 'Someone who's being . . . controlled. That's what you're saying.'

Jasmine just looked at him.

'But there's just one problem with that, isn't there?' said Ben. 'And I'm sorry' – he grinned again – 'but it's a real stumbling block for me. Everyone else we've seen who's been bitten has got one of these things on *the back of their neck.*' He paused. 'Now, if we're talking about *control*, the back of the neck does kind of make sense. Something back there' – he clapped a hand to the back of his own neck – 'could mess around with the signals coming out of your brain – the spinal cord or whatever. But if you're telling me that there's someone in there' – he pointed at the door to the other room – 'who's secretly working against us, who's a traitor, but *doesn't* have one of these things on the back of their neck – well, for one thing, where do you reckon they actually have it?' He looked at her, still grinning.

'I don't know,' said Jasmine. 'It's . . . somewhere else. Under their clothes somewhere, I guess.' She was getting really infuriated now, not only at Ben and his grin (and she'd thought it was cute!) but at how weak what she was saying actually sounded.

Maybe she was wrong. Jasmine hated being wrong.

'Maybe the crawlers don't have to bite you on the neck,' she said. 'Maybe they can still control you from some other part of your body. How should I know?'

Ben kept grinning at her. *Any second now she's going to realize she's sounding crazy*, he thought. *We're going to have a laugh about this. Any second now.*

Jasmine gave him a long look. 'It's easy to pick holes in other people's ideas,' she said, 'when you don't come up with any of your own.'

Ben blinked.

'I didn't ask you to believe me,' Jasmine told him. 'I just thought you'd appreciate some kind of warning. *Watch who you're with*, that's all I'm saying. You're right: I don't have any evidence. But I don't see why that makes you feel you can stand there with that' – she scowled – 'that *smug grin* on your face!'

The grin had gone now. Ben's mouth hung open.

'I . . . I didn't mean—' he managed.

Jasmine raised a hand to interrupt him. 'Excuse me, but

– you know what? On second thoughts I'll watch the screens by myself.'

She turned her back on him and sat down facing the monitors.

After a moment she heard the door click shut behind her.

10:08 PM.

So that was how Ben found himself kicked out of the monitor room for the second time in less than half an hour. Only, instead of continuing to get on the wrong side of Josh, this time he seemed to have blown things completely with Jasmine.

What she'd said about him being 'smug' had stung him badly. He was all too aware of the privileges of his fee-paying education. He *did* go to a posh school – and, to his shame, some kids at that school did think less of people who weren't so lucky. That was why Ben had flinched when Josh had called Samantha a 'pleb'. It was exactly the kind of obnoxious, arrogant attitude that he most hated to be associated with. And now Jasmine had apparently classed him squarely in the same category.

Standing once again with his back to the monitor-room door, he looked at the rest of the group.

Robert and Hugo were simply staring into space. Ben supposed they must have zoned out; gone into some kind of mental holding pattern while they waited to be rescued. But their expressions, he noticed, were every bit as eerily blank and vacant as those on the faces of the adults outside.

The silent, mousey girl – Ben had almost forgotten her name again . . . *Lisa*, that was it – just sat on her chair. Her hair still hung over her face and she was still hugging her knees, rocking herself back and forth, again and again.

Samantha and Lauren were huddled over their phones, whispering about something.

And lolling in a chair, looking up at Ben, was Josh.

'Back with us so soon?' Josh asked – with what Ben considered a textbook example of the ultimate 'smug grin'.

'Er—' said Ben. But he was saved from having to think up some lame excuse for why he wasn't next door with Jasmine by a sudden interruption.

An explosion of sound resolved into beats. There was a bar of tinny keyboard intro from a mobile phone's built-in speaker. Then Samantha and Lauren started to sing.

'*OOOOOOOH baby babe . . .*' they crooned, then looked at each other and burst into giggles as everyone turned to stare at them.

'Er . . . 'scuse me?' said Hugo, who'd turned round in his chair.

'*OOOOOOOOH baby babe,*' they both sang, '*I'm a slave to your love!*'

'Excuse me,' Hugo repeated. 'Do you mind?'

'Mind what?' Samantha asked innocently. The music continued, sounding incredibly loud after all the relative quiet in the room. Lauren too had stopped singing, but her grin was wide and her eyes gleamed in gleeful anticipation.

'The music,' said Hugo.

'What about it?'

'Could you *turn it off*, please?'

'Why?'

'Because it's rubbish?' Hugo suggested.

Samantha's eyes widened as she pretended to look shocked for a moment. Then she shrugged. 'That's just your opinion.'

Hugo stared at her, nonplussed, as the music continued. Samantha stared straight back.

'Look,' he managed eventually, 'I really, *really* don't want to have to listen to this stuff.'

'Cover your ears then,' said Samantha.

Hugo blinked. 'You . . . you're not the only person in the room, you know!' he spluttered.

'Well spotted,' said Samantha serenely. 'So?'

'So . . . why should the rest of us have to put up with your horrible racket?'

'Why should we have to turn our music off?' Samantha asked back. 'Just because *you* say so?'

'But . . . can't you listen to it on headphones or something?'

'Don't have none,' said Samantha, still staring at him.

It was a challenge, Ben realized. This was a game that Samantha had obviously played many times before. And now it was Hugo's move.

What could he do? Ben watched Hugo's face as the possibilities slowly percolated through the brain behind it. He could try to grab the phone from the girls, but that was very physical: Hugo was reluctant to push things that far. Ben watched him look to Josh for guidance.

But Josh shook his head.

Now Ben could see that Hugo was *really* confused. Hugo always relied on Josh. But while being mates with Josh might count for something at their school, apparently that meant nothing here.

Hugo was out of his element. He was helpless.

'Well, I think it's very selfish of you!' he said finally.

Samantha's grin was triumphant.

Ben just watched. An ugly thought had occurred to him.

He was in the same position as Hugo, he realized; worse, probably. He knew next to nothing about the people in the room with him. Even the ones from his own school weren't much more than strangers to him – or enemies. And yet here they all were, trapped together, reacting to the situation in their various unpredictable personal ways.

What if Jasmine was right? he thought. What if one – or more! – of the group *had* been secretly bitten and taken over? Suddenly it didn't seem like such a ridiculous idea after all, for one simple reason:

How would he know?

10:10 PM.

The door to the monitor room was solid and fitted well in its frame: when Ben had closed it behind him Jasmine was sealed off from the rest of the group. For the first time, she was alone. Her shoulders sagged with relief.

She did feel a little bad about kicking Ben out. *OK*, she admitted to herself, *maybe more than a little.* But the silence of his absence felt blissful. For a few minutes at least she didn't have to put up a front any more. At last she could give in to what she was really feeling.

For more than two hours now Jasmine had been busying her mind with what was happening, working out what to do about it. She'd made herself concentrate on each moment as it came, examining every detail, wringing out all the information she could. It had been a good strategy, because behind all that cool analysis her ears still rang with screams.

Jasmine was scared. Horribly, desperately scared.

This wasn't, she knew, a question of cowardice or weakness.

While it was true that the boys – or Josh, Hugo and Ben at any rate – seemed, on the outside, to be relatively unfazed by their situation, Jasmine knew that wasn't because they were stronger than her. *It was because they weren't thinking clearly.*

They believed they were going to be rescued – that it was only a question of waiting. This comforting certainty had taken the place of any further rational examination of the situation. Jasmine could see why: the possibility that they *weren't* going to be rescued was too grim to contemplate.

She looked at the time-code at the corner of the nearest monitor. If the evening had gone according to schedule the play would be nearing its end. Before much longer, she and Ms Gresham and the other girls would have been on their way home. The gulf between that outcome and what had actually taken place seemed impossible to reconcile.

How had it happened? How had she ended up trapped with a load of kids she hardly knew while the rest of the building went mad? What were the crawlers? Where had they come from? *Why was this happening to them?*

Sudden movement on the monitors snapped her out of her reverie.

No less than four police vans had arrived: the feed from the camera that covered the Barbican's main entrance was flickering with their revolving lights. As Jasmine watched, the vans' doors slid back, spilling out black-clad men in helmets carrying batons and shields.

Riot police.

Jasmine reached forward and started punching buttons on the console in front of the monitors. Obediently their contents began to change and swap as they showed the feeds from different cameras all over the building. The view of the frozen sentries out in the passageway vanished, settling instead on one she hadn't seen before: this camera must be positioned on the foyer ceiling. It looked down on a spot not far from the main street entrance.

At first the police were visible only as a growing shadow against the glass. But not for long. Two of them shoulder-charged the doors, then they all burst into the foyer. They locked shields and formed a phalanx, batons raised.

It was weird seeing the scene unfold in silence – scarier, somehow. There were maybe thirty riot police on the screen but all Jasmine could hear was the sound of her own breathing.

She got halfway out of the chair to tell the others what was happening – but then she noticed more movement on another of the monitors. A hard ball of ice-cold fear formed in her chest.

'Oh, no . . .' she whispered.

On one, two, three of the screens now Jasmine could see people sneaking into position, massing in the foyer's surrounding passages. Each one of them moved with eerie precision, following exactly the footsteps of the person in front of them. Each had an indistinct but unmistakable shape on the back of their neck.

At the same time Jasmine noticed a strange, spreading blur on the stretch of concrete wall over the main doors – over the heads of the police. This wasn't something wrong with the screen: *it was more crawlers.*

The police were walking into another trap. And there was no way to warn them.

All at once, baring their teeth in identical snarls of rage, hundreds of people burst from their hiding places and charged at the ring of riot police from all directions.

Jasmine watched in silence.

Ordinary men and women – middle-class, culture-loving adults dressed in suits and dresses and overcoats and cardigans – were now storming across the carpeted foyer like ravening beasts. The police barely had time to brace themselves before the first of them crunched into the ring of shields, which vanished under a scrum of pressing bodies, screaming faces and flailing, grasping limbs.

The police apparently couldn't quite bring themselves to hit their opponents. Instead they held their sticks crosswise to try to fend off the crowd. But their circle squeezed inexorably inward. Slowly they were being pushed back.

When they were in range, the crawlers dropped on them.

One by one, the police stopped fighting and started slapping at themselves. An officer in the centre suddenly froze in place, standing completely rigid before collapsing.

Then the ring of shields broke. The crowd surged through.

Again, it happened very fast. One or two black-clad figures remained standing for a few seconds more, brandishing their batons, but threats, even blows, had no effect. In moments all the hapless riot cops were on the floor – forced to the ground and held down while the crawlers did their work. The crowd piled on top of them, grabbing arms and legs, yanking off helmets. Soon the last of the invaders was subdued.

Now, at last, the crowd pulled back. Their frenzy was gone. Their hands had stopped clutching and flailing and grabbing, and had fallen to their sides. Now they were waiting.

One by one the fallen riot police got up again. One by one – eyes glassy and staring, movements awkward and puppet-like at first – they joined the surrounding crowd. Without speaking, or even acknowledging each other, the crowd dispersed. Pausing only to pick up the discarded shields, helmets, armour and other equipment that were the only evidence of the battle that had just taken place, they set off in the various directions from which they had come.

The screens emptied of people, leaving bare carpet and deserted corridors.

So much for getting rescued.

10:22 PM.

'Here,' said Samantha suddenly as the music continued. 'Can you smell something?'

While Ben, Robert, Josh and Hugo sniffed the air, Lisa stopped rocking herself.

'No,' said Josh.

'What?' said Ben. He noticed that Lauren had started smiling.

'There's a weird smell in here,' said Samantha. 'Seriously. I think it's getting stronger.'

'What kind of smell?' said Hugo.

'I don't know,' said Samantha, 'but I think it smells a bit like . . . wee.'

Lauren made a snorking sound in her nose, then burst out laughing.

Samantha sniffed once, then grimaced. 'Yeah,' she said, nod-ding, 'there's a definite whiff of wee in here. Can't you smell it?'

The boys looked at each other uncertainly.

'It's almost,' said Samantha, 'as if someone's *wet themselves*.'

She turned, casting a suspicious glance at everyone in the room – before finally, exaggeratedly, settling on Lisa.

Under her fringe of hair Lisa jerked her face to one side as if she'd been slapped.

Lauren laughed like a hyena.

Ben frowned. He really couldn't smell anything. But then, of course, he realized . . .

'*Has* anyone wet themselves?' asked Samantha. 'No?' she added with heavy emphasis when nobody answered. 'Oh. Then it must be *you*, Lisa.'

Lisa said nothing, just sat frozen on her chair.

Samantha started to smile – the kind of smile a cat might make while torturing a mouse.

'Lisa has these *accidents* sometimes,' she said. 'She doesn't mean to, but she just can't help it. It's a bit embarrassing, so don't be mean to her about it, but I thought you boys should know. If something starts to smell a bit *pissy* in here, don't worry. It's only Lisa.'

Ben and the other boys said nothing. What could they say? Ben felt his face going red and he didn't know where to look. The worst thing was, he knew that the lack of reaction would make poor Lisa think that everyone was taking Samantha's words at face value.

The song from Samantha's phone came to an end. There was a short and terrible silence then Lisa stood up, clasping

her school bag in front of her. She walked to the door of the
monitor room.

There was no smell. Ben noticed nothing as Lisa went past.
But—

'Funny,' said Samantha as the music started up again. 'The
smell's not so strong now.'

Lauren laughed until her eyes were wet with tears.

10:24 PM.

Jasmine heard a burst of laughter and music, which was
muffled to silence again as the door snicked shut behind her.
She turned.

'Oh,' she said, surprised. 'Hi, Lisa. What's going on?'

Lisa just shook her head.

Jasmine looked at her. It was obvious what had happened:
Samantha and Lauren had been pulling their routines on Lisa
ever since Jasmine had known them. But she, like Ben, had
sat silent when it first happened, and now too much time had
passed: if she said anything about it to Lisa now it would look
too much like pity, and that, Jasmine knew, might make things
even worse.

'You just missed something big,' she said instead, as casually
as she could, turning in the chair and gesturing at the monitors
as Lisa came up behind her. 'Riot police actually baton-charged

the place a minute ago, but you'd never know to look at it out there now . . .'

She glanced back at Lisa – and froze.

Lisa's right hand, Jasmine saw, had just come out of her school bag. The hand was holding the missing crawler – one of the ones that had been stepped on earlier. Lisa's fingers were clasped firmly around its partially crushed body, and the creature's legs were twitching and pulsing with what was definitely some kind of life.

Jasmine gaped.

Behind her curtain of hair Lisa's glassy eyes narrowed. Realizing she'd been caught, her thin lips parted in a silent snarl of fury. She dropped the bag and her left hand loomed in Jasmine's vision: the hand clamped over Jasmine's mouth, fingers digging into her cheeks, stifling her scream before she'd even thought to utter one.

With her right hand, the one holding the crawler, Lisa lunged.

Jasmine flung up her own hands, catching hold of Lisa's wrist. She was almost too late: the twitching creature was just centimetres from her face. Its five legs – broken and disjointed but hideously eager – grasped for her. Twin needles of bone, glistening with fluid, flickered in and out from the crawler's centre mass. For a long second Jasmine managed to hold Lisa there, keeping her off. Then, snarl widening into a grin of triumph, Lisa pushed harder.

It was all happening so fast, Jasmine barely had time to be frightened. Even now, as she fought, the analytical part of her mind coldly noted the grim reality of the situation: Lisa's surprise attack had, essentially, worked. She had the drop on Jasmine, who was twisted round on her seat. Lisa, standing behind her, could bear down on her victim with her whole bodyweight. Jasmine resisted with all her strength but it was hopeless: Lisa's left hand was clawing at her face and the right, with its grisly burden, was coming closer.

Jasmine slid down on the chair, which revolved and dumped her, still clasping Lisa's wrists, onto the floor. But Lisa just came with her, bending over her, forcing the crawler down towards her.

Jasmine's blood hammered in her ears. Her vision narrowed. Her world closed in around the creature until there was nothing else left.

With a last, desperate effort, she kicked out at the door.

10:25 PM.

'What was that?' asked Ben, over the sound of more music from Samantha's phone.

'What was what, now?' Josh asked back, annoyed.

'I thought I heard something.'

'I'm surprised anyone can hear anything with this racket,' grumbled Hugo.

'No, really,' said Ben. 'There was a thump. I think it came from next door. I'm going to check on Jasmine.'

'I'll bet,' said Samantha, and Lauren *snorked* again – which distracted Ben for a crucial second as he got the door open.

'Whoa,' he managed.

From Ben's perspective Lisa and Jasmine were lying across the doorway, one on top of the other. Lisa's face twisted round: her curtain of hair parted and her staring eyes met his. Without pausing her attack on Jasmine for a moment, she let out a screech.

'*Eeeeeeeeeeeh!*'

'Oh crap!' said Ben.

Numbly, his movements feeling horribly slow and uncertain, he grabbed for Lisa's arm, her right, the one holding the crawler – and pulled.

Lisa's arm was small and thin but her muscles felt like steel hawsers. Ben heaved back, and succeeded in lifting the crawler away from Jasmine a little, but even with her upward force added to his own he was fighting Lisa for every millimetre. She was still shrieking: her head thrashed from side to side, whipping flecks of foaming spittle in all directions.

'Uh, help?' said Ben.

'Get out of the way!' Hugo bellowed back, shouldering past him through the narrow doorway.

Ben, knocked sideways, lost his grip. But now, for once, Hugo was taking charge. He bent down, hooked his beefy arms under Lisa's, and – with a strength that left Ben staring – hauled the struggling girl upright, off Jasmine, and back through the door into the main room.

'Grab her arms,' he grunted as he lowered Lisa to the floor. Robert and Josh did as he said, pinning them out from her body. Still Lisa struggled. Still she twitched and thrashed and bucked. Ben just stared.

'Get on her legs, Ben!' warned Hugo, snapping him out of it. 'Sit on 'em. Quick!'

When the four boys had finally managed to restrain Lisa, there was a pause.

'So,' Jasmine asked Ben shakily, from beside him. 'You *still* don't believe me about a traitor in the group?'

Ben just looked at her.

Jasmine could have milked the moment. She could have made more of being proved right, and how much danger she'd just been in. But crowing wasn't her style.

'Are you all right, Jasmine?' asked Hugo, before Ben remembered to do so – making Ben feel like even more of a spare part than he did already.

'I'm fine,' Jasmine lied, feeling her face and wondering

if the marks of Lisa's fingers were still visible. Then she noticed that everyone was looking at her again.

'Well,' she added, gathering herself with an effort, 'first things first . . .'

Both Hugo and Robert were kneeling on Lisa's right arm, keeping the arm straight out from her body, but the hand still held its burden: the crawler's legs were still twitching.

'There was a bin in here earlier,' said Jasmine, snapping her fingers. 'That rubbish bin, the metal one – anyone seen it?'

'Here,' said Robert, pointing. Hugo nodded to indicate he had Lisa's arm under control himself for now, so Robert stood up, grabbed the bin, and made to pass it to Jasmine.

'OK,' said Jasmine. 'Robert, isn't it?'

Robert nodded.

'Turn the bin upside-down and put it over Lisa's hand – the one with the crawler. Quickly now. We don't want her suddenly trying to throw it at us or something.'

Looking extremely dubious, Robert did as Jasmine asked, squatting down on the floor. Now the rim of the metal bin lay against Lisa's wrist. Lisa's hand and the crawler were concealed beneath it. All the while Lisa's head continued to lash from side to side.

'That's good, Robert, thank you,' said Jasmine. 'Now, no matter what happens next, I want you to be ready and watching. If Lisa lets go – if the crawler even *tries* to escape – I want you to trap it and make sure it doesn't get out. OK?'

Robert nodded again.

'All right,' said Jasmine wearily, 'then I guess it's time to find out if the rest of my theory was true too.'

Except for the snarling sounds that Lisa was still making, the room was now silent. Everyone in the group was either staring at Lisa or watching Jasmine, hanging on whatever she was going to say next.

'I need a volunteer,' she announced. 'Samantha? Lauren? It's got to be one of you.'

'Why?' asked Josh.

'We have to assume that what's happened to Lisa isn't her fault. We've got to treat her with whatever respect we can. Because now . . .' Jasmine paused. 'Now we've got to search her.'

'No problem,' said Samantha, stepping forward.

Lisa froze. She fixed Samantha with a stare, bared her teeth, and her snarling sank to a low growl in her throat.

'Where do I start?' Samantha asked.

Jasmine bit her lip. But it had to be done. 'Lisa's blouse,' she said. 'Open it from the bottom buttons first. But *carefully*,' she emphasized. 'We don't know what you might find.'

Samantha nodded. Reaching a hand to either side of Lisa's waist she tugged at the blouse, gently untucking the white material until it came free of the waistband of Lisa's pleated grey school skirt. Then she unfastened the bottom button.

And stopped.

'Oh,' said Lauren, looking down over Samantha's shoulder. 'Oh, that's just . . . *wrong.*'

The blouse had parted to reveal, not Lisa's stomach, but something else. Its rubbery, semi-translucent flesh was a parody of Lisa's skin. Its long legs with their thin lines of red at the joints quivered slightly, as if it knew that its secret had been discovered.

It was another crawler, squatting on Lisa's belly.

10:31 PM.

Ben – still sitting on Lisa's legs – stared at the creature, utterly revolted. He thought of the way Lisa had been behaving earlier in the evening when he'd last noticed her: the way she'd been rocking back and forth, her arms wrapped around herself. Herself, and the thing that controlled her.

'But,' said Samantha, 'that means it must've had its teeth in her the whole time!'

'That's horrible!' wailed Lauren.

'That's *rank*!' agreed Samantha.

'That must be the way these things work,' put in Jasmine, trying to keep everyone on track. 'Maybe they bite you on the back of the neck if they can. But if they need to hide, if they need not to be seen, then . . .' She gestured downwards.

There was a long silence.

'But what are we going to do with her?' asked Josh. 'We can't just . . . *keep* her like that – can we?'

'I tell you,' said Hugo. 'She's a lot stronger than she looks.'

'We could tie her up,' said Lauren.

'What with?' asked Ben.

'I can hear you, you know,' said Lisa, making everyone jump. She grinned up at them, shook her head, and in a completely normal voice said: 'Idiots.'

Everybody looked at each other.

'You can't resist her,' Lisa told them. 'In fact, why do you even want to?'

Nobody answered. Looking at Lisa, nobody knew what to say.

'She has *given me strength*,' said Lisa. 'She has taken all my weakness and my hate and she has turned it into love. That's why I did what I did. That's why I want to stop you trying to fight her – because I love you.' She smiled. 'Yes, even *you*, Samantha. I love all of you, because *she* loves me.'

'Who?' said Jasmine. 'Who are you talking about?'

'The Queen,' said Lisa. Tears trembled at the corners of her eyes. 'The Queen loves each and every one of us. Soon you will all feel her love, the way I do. I'd do anything for the Queen. Anything. And soon,' she repeated, 'so will you.'

'This is too weird now,' said Lauren. 'This is freaking me out. I don't want to hear it. Make it stop!' she shouted, pointing at Lisa.

Samantha reached down.

'Wait!' said Jasmine. 'No!'

Samantha grabbed the crawler and pulled it from Lisa's body. With a soft, wet sound that Ben found unforgettably repulsive its long twin probosces came after it.

The creature's legs were now dangling from between Samantha's fingers, twitching. Samantha looked thoroughly disgusted. But Lisa's eyes had now rolled up in their sockets. She lay there like a discarded rag doll.

Hugo put a hand to Lisa's neck.

'Is she . . . ?' asked Jasmine.

'She's breathing. Pulse is slow, but steady,' said Hugo. He sat back, looked at Jasmine and shrugged bleakly. 'I learned first aid with the cadets,' he explained. 'But she needs a doctor really.'

'Great,' said Jasmine, infuriated. 'Great!' She rounded on Samantha. 'What were you thinking? You could have killed her!'

'And Lisa tried to put one of these things on you,' Samantha reminded her, gesturing with the crawler. Held from behind, its rubbery legs grasped at the empty air. 'Now, where shall I put this? Unless *you'd* like to hold it for a while?'

'Throw it out,' said Josh. 'Throw them *all* out. Frankly,' he added, shuddering as he stood up, 'I don't know what we thought we were doing trying to keep the vile things in the first place.'

'I agree,' said Robert, with feeling, from beside his wastepaper basket, which was still upturned over Lisa's hand.

'Slinging 'em out's got my vote,' said Samantha.

'Too right,' said Lauren.

'Wait a second, though,' said Ben, standing up too. 'Throw them out *where*? Where are we going to put them, exactly?'

'The passage, of course!' snapped Josh. 'It's not like there's anywhere else they can go, and it's too dangerous to keep them any longer.'

'But it's dangerous to open the door,' said Ben, 'isn't it? Maybe you forgot, but there's a whole load of adults out there. What's to stop them rushing us?'

'We'll keep the barricades close to the door, obviously,' said Josh. 'We'll just lift them for a minute, open the door just wide enough, then slam it shut again with the lockers back behind it. Job done.' He shrugged. 'What's your problem?'

'My problem is that it's a big risk,' said Ben. 'I think we should discuss it first.'

Josh rolled his eyes and gave a short sigh. 'Fine,' he said. 'By all means, let's *discuss* it. But I will say this: there's no point hesitating just because we're *scared*.'

He stared straight into Ben's eyes, and smirked.

Ben gaped at him. This really was classic Josh. There were a number of methods that he used to secure his position as ruler of their school year, but humiliation – making anyone who disagreed with him appear to be doing so simply out of some kind of weakness – had always been Josh's favourite.

'I'm not scared,' said Ben.

'Really,' said Josh drily. 'It's odd you say that, because I seem to remember you making the same kind of fuss when the crawlers were trying to climb *in*.' He paused, grinning at Samantha and Lauren who (Ben was annoyed to notice) grinned straight back. 'When we came to help you before there was nothing there, remember?' He sneered. 'Well, maybe this won't be as bad as you're making out, either.'

'I'm not standing around holding this thing all night,' said Samantha, 'that's for sure.'

'You tell 'im, babes,' said Lauren.

'I . . .' Ben tried again – but he felt a touch on his arm: Jasmine.

'All right,' she said coolly. 'I agree. Let's get rid of them. They've caused enough trouble. But then we need a proper discussion about whatever we're going to do after that. Right?'

'Of course,' said Josh, all politeness. 'OK, everyone, time to get organized. First, let's get all these horrors together and accounted for. Which reminds me: what, dare I ask, has happened to the other two that Jasmine was examining?'

Ben blinked. He'd been so wrapped up in the business with Lisa that he'd completely forgotten about them. He wasn't the only one, either, as he could tell from the worried looks from Lauren and Robert.

He checked the sink. Relief.

'They're in here.'

'Well that's something, at least,' said Josh. 'Wouldn't want any more of them to go walkabout, would we?' Still looking at Ben, he grinned nastily. 'Pick 'em up, Freeman.'

'What?' said Ben.

'Pick them up,' Josh repeated. 'Unless you're still feeling scared, of course?'

'Sure,' said Ben, doing his best to smile back and hide his fury. 'No problem.'

He looked back at the sink's contents, and gulped. He'd already seen one of these creatures come back to life. He had no wish to risk it happening again while he was holding one himself – let alone two.

But Josh was waiting behind him, along with Jasmine and everyone else: there was no backing out now. He reached in over the sink's stained chrome sides.

The crawlers' flesh was rubbery beneath his fingertips: it squidged a little as he touched them. Their skin, he noticed, was faintly waxy, almost damp. The urge just to hurl the creatures away and scrub their contact traces off him was almost unbearable. But – keeping carefully clear of their undersides, where the proboscees were – Ben forced his fingers to close around the bodies and take their weight. Composing his face into a mask of outward calm he lifted them both clear of the sink and turned back to face Josh.

'All right,' he said, as casually as he could, 'where do you want 'em?'

'We could stick them in the bin,' put in Hugo before Josh could answer. 'Get them all in there, like a bucket. Open the door, toss the bin out, shut the door again.'

'That's got to make more sense than throwing them out one at a time,' said Ben (and not just, he told himself, because it meant he wouldn't have to hold the crawlers any longer than necessary). 'I mean, we want that door open for the minimum amount of time possible – right?'

'Good idea,' said Josh to Hugo. Then: 'Robert?'

'Oh,' said Robert. 'Right.' Blinking rapidly, licking his lips, he gingerly righted the upside-down bin. Revealed again, the crawler on Lisa's palm twitched one of its broken legs, making it loll horribly. But Robert picked it up by a leg and, shuddering, dropped it in.

Samantha's followed it.

'Now yours, Freeman.'

This was one order from Josh that Ben was glad to follow: his two crawlers went into the bin. Then he rubbed his hands on the sides of his scratchy school trousers, hard.

'Right,' said Josh, looking at the bin's contents with distaste. 'Who'll volunteer to carry them?'

'I'll do it,' said Hugo, getting up.

'Good man,' said Josh. 'Then let's get these lockers shifted. Freeman? Robert?'

'Hold on,' said Jasmine. 'Don't you think we ought to have someone check what's going on in the passage on the cameras first?'

'Whatever,' said Lauren, rolling her eyes.

'Let's just get these things out of here, yeah?' said Samantha.

'Fine,' said Jasmine. 'I'll go check the cameras then. Give me a second.'

But as soon as she was through the door, she realized there was a problem.

'Well?' called Josh from the other room. 'What can you see? What's going on out there?'

'I . . . I can't tell,' Jasmine admitted.

'What? Why not?'

'Because,' said Jasmine, 'I changed what's on the screens.

And now . . .' She stabbed at the buttons fruitlessly. The screens in front of her cycled through the views from hundreds of cameras all over the Barbican complex. But they stubbornly refused to show the one she wanted.

'Now you can't get the view of the passage back,' said Josh, from behind her. *'Brilliant.'*

Startled, Jasmine turned. Josh's face was full of contempt.

'What did Hugo say?' he asked. *'What did we say?'*

'Er . . .' said Jasmine.

'We told you and Freeman not to *touch* anything!'

'What? Look, there were riot police a minute ago. I wanted to see what was going on.'

'I don't care! You should've asked first!'

'Why?' asked Jasmine, getting annoyed.

'Because,' said Josh, 'like it or not, *I'm in charge*. You and Freeman, you're as bad as each other! You're a – a bloody *menace*, the pair of you!'

'Um, Josh?' called Hugo from the other room, before Jasmine could reply.

'What is it *now*?'

'It's the crawlers, mate,' said Hugo. 'They're moving again.'

'For God's sake . . .' Josh turned on his heel and left the monitor room. Giving up on the console for the time being, Jasmine came after him.

Hugo was standing in the centre of the room, holding the bin. 'They're waking up, mate,' he said. His voice was calm but his eyes betrayed his tension, and the truth of his words was underlined by the fact that at that moment the tips of two of the crawlers' legs were just beginning to protrude over the lip of the bin.

They were trying to climb out.

Lauren made a whimpering sound and backed away.

'All right,' said Josh, 'we'll have to chance it. Freeman? Robert? Get ready to shift those lockers when I say. Hugo, you get near the door. Be ready to chuck those things out as soon as it opens.'

'No problem,' said Hugo, with feeling.

'Then let's do this,' said Josh.

Frowning with effort, Ben and Robert lifted the lockers from the door.

Everyone fell silent – waiting and watching. Ben had been half expecting the door to burst inward as soon as their improvised barricade was removed but, for now, it was still.

'Here we go,' Hugo murmured, stepping forward. Taking one hand off the bucket, he reached past the lockers to the door handle.

There was enough space for the door to open about a foot. Robert and Ben were poised behind the lockers. The view out of the door was blocked for everyone else by Hugo himself.

'How's it look out there?' asked Josh.

'They're still there,' said Hugo, in a low whisper. 'Still . . . frozen. Just standing there, like statues.'

'Don't let nothing else in,' murmured Lauren softly, from behind him.

'Don't hang about, mate,' Josh agreed. 'Just chuck the bin out and let's get this over with, eh?'

'Right,' said Hugo.

Everyone held their breath. Hugo swung his hands back towards himself, then swung them forward.

But just when he was about to let go and throw the bin and what was inside it as far away as he could:

'Oh,' he said. 'One of them's . . .'

'What?' asked Josh.

For a second more Hugo stood there, his eyes widening, his arms still sticking straight out of the door. Then, with brutal suddenness, he disappeared from sight.

He'd been yanked out of the room.

'HUGO!' Shock pushed Josh's voice up to a shrill squeak, which was drowned out by a piercing scream from Lauren.

Ben just stared, stunned, at the place where Hugo had been standing. Hugo might not be too hot on taking the initiative, but over the evening he had proved to be one of the stronger and braver people in the group. With his loss, hysteria spread through the room until the air seemed to ripple with it.

Everyone yelled, swore, shouted Hugo's name.

In answer, a forest of arms reached in around the side of the door. They seemed to sprout from the gap, thrashing like tentacles: hands whipped wildly for purchase, snatching at whatever they could find. At the same instant, Ben, Robert and the barricade lockers were all rocked back by a concerted shove from outside.

'The door!' shrieked Jasmine. '*Shut the door!*'

At last Josh lunged, adding his weight to that of Robert and Ben. The wall of lockers toppled forward.

It stopped before the door could be closed again. Too many arms had been pushed through the gap. They were crushed there in a bunch; the arms' owners – if they cared – would have some horrible bruises, maybe worse. But the door was still open. The hands were still grasping gamely. Even with the three boys pushing them, the lockers began to rock back again under the pressure on the door from outside. And as if all that wasn't enough—

'Robert, *look out*!' Jasmine warned.

Three, four, five hands snaked around the edge of the door and grabbed hold of Robert's left side – three taking his arm, one latching onto his waistband, one snatching at his leg. Their knuckles whitened.

'Wha—?' said Robert. He staggered sideways round the side of the lockers. With the loss of his weight and strength the barricade lurched upright. Then the lockers were tipping back into the room. As well as the adults pushing from outside Ben and Josh were now struggling against the weight of the barricade itself.

While Lauren just kept screaming, Jasmine stepped forward and grabbed Robert's other arm. And Samantha . . .

'Gaaaaaaaah!'

Bellowing, Samantha launched herself bodily against the barricade – and everyone and everything else in her way.

'AHH!' There was an answering yelp of agony from Robert. Samantha's charge had occurred at the exact moment when his left arm was sticking out through the gap in the door: the combined weight of Ben, Robert, Samantha and the lockers crunched into it behind the door's hard edge – and stopped there, as the door failed to shut for a second time.

'Get out! Get out! Get out!' shrieked Samantha, smashing into Ben, the locker, Robert's arm, everything, again and again. Twice more the door failed to close. But on the last 'Get out!' several things happened at once.

The hands holding Robert let go. He fell back, taking Jasmine with him; the two of them hit the floor in a heap. Something similar must have been happening outside because the hands in the doorway retreated for a crucial moment. The door slammed shut. The lockers fell back against it with a crash.

Then there was silence.

10:49 pm.

'How – how did that happen?' asked Samantha, panting, pointing at the door. She looked around the room, eyes wide, waiting for an answer. 'What just happened there? Can anyone tell me?'

'I guess they were waiting for us,' said Jasmine, sitting on the floor.

'You "guess",' Samantha echoed.

Jasmine shrugged, too numb to face an argument. 'Who can say for sure?'

Samantha scowled. 'You know what, Jasmine? I've heard enough words from you for one night. I don't want to hear any more "I guess" – not from you, not from anybody. I want to hear some facts, and I want to hear them now. *What the hell are we going to do?* How are we going to get out of this? I mean, one second that boy was standing there by the door, and then . . .' She lashed out at the lockers with her foot: *blam!*

Everyone flinched.

'We're getting picked off here – that's *two* of us down now. Who's going to be next, do you think? *Who's next?*'

'OK, Samantha,' said Josh, 'that's enough.'

'*What* did you say?' said Samantha heavily, rounding on Josh, eyes flashing.

'I said, that's enough.'

'No,' said Samantha, pointing at Josh and smiling mirthlessly. 'No, no – *you* don't get to say anything. I mean, whose idea was it to open the door in the first place? Who sent him out there? *Whose fault is it that Hugo's gone?*'

'Now – now just wait a second . . .' Josh stammered. 'We all agreed we wanted to get rid of the crawlers, right?'

Nobody answered.

'We *all agreed*,' he repeated, with great emphasis. 'You can't turn round now and say it's my fault. You just can't!'

Still nobody spoke. Everyone was staring at Josh – Ben included. He had never before seen Josh look less than completely confident and certain. But now . . .

'How was I to know that was going to happen?' asked Josh. His voice had gone high and scratchy, and his lower lip was trembling. 'How was I to know they were going to grab him like that?' He shook his head. 'It's not my fault! It's not! *It's not my fault!*'

Josh's shout seemed to echo in the tiny space of the room. His handsome face was creased with misery. His cheeks were red. He was blinking back tears. For another long second he just stood there. Then, to Ben's astonishment, he ran into the monitor room, banging the door shut behind him.

The end of Josh's leadership should, Ben supposed, have made him happy. But it didn't – he just felt sick and empty inside. They'd lost Hugo; Lisa still lay unconscious on the floor where she'd been left; now Josh had gone to pieces. Samantha was right: who was going to be next?

'My arm,' said Robert. 'I . . . I think it's broken.'

'You're kidding,' said Samantha in disbelief.

Robert looked at her. 'No,' he said heavily, 'I'm not. And I don't know why *you're* so surprised. After all, it was you who kept slamming it in the door.'

He had sat up on the floor, cradling his left arm with his right. Slowly, grimacing, Robert took his right hand away, revealing the sleeve of his white school uniform shirt, now red with blood. 'I can't move my fingers,' he said.

Ben could see why. They were swollen and they had gone a strange grey colour too.

'Oh my God!' said Lauren helpfully, pointing.

'Well, does anyone know first aid?' asked Jasmine.

'Anyone *else*, you mean,' corrected Ben.

Jasmine fell silent, as did the rest of the room, again, as they thought about Hugo. He had known first aid. And this probably wasn't going to be the last time that his skills or his strength were going to be missed.

'Well,' said Jasmine, forcing her thoughts back to practicalities, 'I guess first of all we need to clean the wound. Then we'll need bandages of some kind, and, um, splints?' She did her best to give Robert a sympathetic smile.

'I don't know first aid, but some sort of sling might help at least—'

'Yeah, there you go again,' said Samantha bitterly. 'And just out of interest, where's all that stuff supposed to come from? We're trapped, stupid!'

'OK, that's it,' said Jasmine, standing up. 'I've heard enough from you, Samantha, and I think the rest of us have too. If you had something constructive or helpful to say then fine, I'd be happy to listen. But you don't, do you? All you can do is stand there fussing.'

'Is that right?'

'Prove me wrong,' said Jasmine. 'Go on, say something useful. You can't – can you? You haven't got a practical thought in your head!'

'Just one,' said Samantha. 'A question. How come you fixed the cameras so we couldn't see what was going on out in the passageway?'

Jasmine blinked. 'What? That wasn't deliberate. I just wanted to—'

'Hugo walked into a trap' – Samantha stepped closer to her – 'because of you. And we're stuck in this room, because of . . . who? Oh yeah: you.'

Jasmine crossed her arms. 'What's your point, Samantha?'

'My point,' said Samantha, 'is that Lisa had a crawler on her the whole time she was in here with us – right? My *point*,' she repeated, getting right up in Jasmine's face, 'is, *what if she wasn't the only one?*'

'Wait a second,' said Jasmine. 'You're telling me that because I chose for us to come in here, and now the screw-up with the cameras, I'm . . . what, Samantha? What are you saying, exactly?'

'Maybe another of us here isn't what they seem,' said Samantha. Having got the rise she wanted out of Jasmine, she was grinning now, triumphant again. 'Maybe there's another traitor in the group. Because the only one of us we can be sure wasn't bitten,' she finished, looking around the room, 'was Hugo.'

10:57 PM.

Without warning the pit was flooded with light.

Mr Miller, the young man whom Steadman had first brought to me, had been in the dark for nearly five hours. His eyes were slow to adjust: I winced at the glare. When I recovered I saw a figure silhouetted on the lip of the pit, looking down.

'What is it, Steadman?' I asked. 'Why are you out of your office?'

In answer, Steadman pointed with his right arm. He was holding something: I only realized what when I heard the shot.

BLAM. Mr Miller went limp: darkness fell for me once more behind his eyes as he died. Then there was a whine of machinery.

I knew that sound. I waited, listening as, slowly, unstoppably, the reinforced glass panel slid back into place above me. Steadman had given me my freedom. Now he was taking it away: he was sealing the pit.

'I am *so* disappointed in you,' he said, his voice sounding strangely small without the speakers. 'All these hundreds of years of the Corporation keeping you captive down here; all these fantastically expensive precautions because we believed you were as powerful as you claimed. And all along you were lying to us.'

I did not reply – which, since Steadman had just killed my nearest mouthpiece, was not surprising. Not possessing, myself, the anatomical extravagance that is a human voice box, I had no way to talk back.

'You know what I think?' Steadman asked. 'I think that in sixteen sixty-six you were *lucky*. Perhaps you got as far as you did because nobody noticed. London did still have the Great Plague to contend with, after all. But now? Today? In this century?' He sniffed. 'You never stood a chance.

'It's been almost five hours since I released you,' he reminded me. 'What have you achieved? You told me you could take over the world, yet so far you've barely managed to take over this building. I mean, really: did you even have a plan? Or were you just going to stay here and hope that everyone on the planet suddenly decided to visit the Barbican? This is a farce. And I'm putting a stop to it.'

I heard footsteps, then an echoing hiss and the rumble of heavy hydraulics.

'I'm opening the door to the sewers,' Steadman announced. 'I'm leaving. If you'd been as good as your word, you could have been coming with me. I thought we could do great things together. With your help, I thought we could put the world to rights – run it properly at last, in an orderly manner, with everyone doing as they're told. Well, *your majesty*, you've wasted enough of my time.

'In just over an hour this building and everything in it will be destroyed. The media will report the explosion as a "terrorist atrocity". I shall be on the other side of the city enjoying a cast-iron alibi and, quite possibly, a splendid dinner. Make no mistake,' Steadman finished, 'I *will* rule the world. But I see that I shall have to do it the only way that counts: with money. Goodbye, *my Queen*.'

That was when we took him.

For almost three hundred and fifty years I had kept certain aspects of my life cycle secret from Steadman and his predecessors. While he'd been talking, two of my new drones had been stalking him.

I had allowed maturation to begin as soon as Steadman had released me. Now, after four hours and forty-something minutes, the drones were almost full-grown. When they dropped from the ceiling above him their weight knocked Steadman to the ground easily. The air rang with the hard, puncturing *thunks* of their ovipositors.

Steadman screamed once. Then, at long last, he shut up.

You see? I did have a plan. It was coming along nicely.

11:01 PM.

For a long time there had been silence. Jasmine and Samantha glared at each other. Robert nursed his arm and grimaced. Ben looked around the room.

Behind him was the door to the monitor room, where Josh was still freaking out in private. To Ben's left was the door through which Hugo had been snatched by the adults standing sentry outside it. To Ben's right lay Lisa, still unconscious.

Ben found himself looking up at the ceiling.

It was made of white plastic tiles, each one about thirty centimetres square. As Ben stared up at them an idea started to form in his mind.

He got up from his spot on the floor and went over to the chair that Hugo had been using, which was now empty. He pushed it along until its back was against the room's third and last set of lockers, which were still standing against the wall. He stood on the seat, put one foot on the top of the chair's back, and straightened his knee. With a certain amount of very uncool scrambling and twisting, he managed to pull himself up.

Now he was lying on top of the lockers, on his back.

'Mind telling me what you think you're doing?' asked Samantha, hand on hip.

'Give me a second,' said Ben. 'I want to try something.'

Reaching his hand up to the nearest of the square plastic ceiling tiles, he pushed at it experimentally.

It lifted. It moved so easily that Ben's entire arm went in with it. The tile tipped from his fingers and fell lightly on top of one of its neighbours.

The space behind it was empty.

Ben blinked. Then, to the ominous creaking of the lockers underneath him, he wriggled and scooted until his head and shoulders lined up with the square hole he'd just created. He took a deep breath, then stuck his head through.

His hunch had turned out to be right. The room's tiled ceiling wasn't its true ceiling at all: the tiles were held up by a grid of some kind of light metal, probably aluminium, behind which there was a gap of another half a metre or so before the concrete underside of the next storey above.

It was dark in there. The light of the room below coming up

around his shoulders didn't penetrate far. In the second or two it took Ben's eyes to adjust he found himself hoping strongly that there was nothing waiting for him in the surrounding shadows. If he was attacked by crawlers now, with his shoulders trapped, he wouldn't stand a chance.

'What's up there? What can you see?' he heard Jasmine ask.

'Shhhhh,' Ben hissed back, making 'keep it down' gestures with his hands, which were still below him in the room. Now he was starting to be able to make out the details he'd been hoping for. To his right, if he turned his head that way, the light from the security room below was now visible to him as a series of faint intersecting lines – the glow escaping weakly around the sides of the ceiling tiles. And to his left . . .

To his left – back towards the lifts – was darkness. The lower half of Ben's body was still lying on top of the lockers: his left arm was pressed against that wall. But up here, above the ceiling tiles, the wall stopped. There was a sort of lip of woolly-looking insulation material sandwiched between two layers of plasterboard, then another grid of ceiling tiles – this one belonging, of course, to the *room next door*.

He gulped. Then he sneezed. It was disgustingly dusty up there. But the fact remained:

'I . . .' he said, hardly believing it. 'I think I've found a way out.'

'What?'

There was a chorus of enquiry and celebration from the room below, and in that second Ben wished he hadn't spoken so soon. Because now, of course, he could see that his 'way out' had major problems. So they could get into the next-door room if they wanted: so what? There were so many sentries outside, the chances were that the door of that room was blocked too. But it was a start.

'Quiet down there,' he told them. 'Let me think.'

After some more wriggling, and a nasty moment when the aluminium frame around him felt like it was cutting into his shoulders and back, he managed to force his arms through the gap so they were up there with him. He pushed down on the tiles to either side of himself – and that was when his suspicions about those were confirmed for him. There was a soft creak, then a *crunch*: the tiles popped out under his weight and fell to the floor below, provoking a squeal of alarm from Lauren. They obviously weren't much stronger if you pushed down on them than if you pushed up – certainly not strong enough to take anyone's full body weight.

Ben paused, thinking, as the sudden uprush of light through the new gap sent purple splashes across his dark-adapted retinas.

Light, he thought. Some part of the ceiling grid had to be stronger than the rest, to support the room's lighting. Craning, wriggling, the frame biting into his back, Ben turned, looking around in the dusty, dark ceiling cavity, searching for what he wanted.

And he found it.

11:04 PM.

'It's a false ceiling,' Ben was explaining. 'There's a gap behind it for wiring and stuff, about this wide.' He held his now somewhat grubby hands apart to demonstrate. 'Most of the ceiling's just made out of these tiles,' he added, pointing at the one on the floor. 'They're not strong enough. But there's this bar thing in the centre that looks much more solid. It goes right through to the next room, maybe even further. And if we can somehow crawl along that, then . . .'

'What?' asked a red-eyed Josh, who had come out of the monitor room to see what was going on.

'Then maybe,' said Jasmine, 'we can work our way far enough along to get away from the sentries outside.' She beamed. 'Nice one, Ben!'

'Thanks,' said Ben. At Jasmine's smile his ears felt very warm all of a sudden. He almost blushed, but—

'No,' said Josh.

'What?' said Ben.

'No,' Josh repeated, shaking his head. 'That's a stupid plan. In fact it's so stupid I don't even think it qualifies as a plan.'

'Why not?'

'Because you don't know how far you'll get! You might get trapped in another room just like this one. More to the point, you might get trapped in one that's not as good as this one – not as safe, or as easy to fortify.'

'It hasn't been all that "safe" so far,' muttered Robert – to Ben's surprise.

'Besides,' Josh went on quickly, 'even if you did get past the sentries, where exactly do you think you'd go after that? How far do you think you're going to get with the whole building riddled with crawlers or people who've been bitten by them? What exactly do you think you're going to achieve,' he added, 'by *abandoning* us like this?'

'What?' said Ben again. 'But . . . what do you mean?'

'Hello?' said Josh. 'Have you thought this through at all?' He pointed at Lisa. 'She's in no shape to come climbing through ceilings with you – and I don't think poor Robert here is, either, do you?'

Pale-faced, Robert cradled his arm and scowled.

'We have to stay with them,' said Josh, with an expression of injured nobility. 'We're going to stay here and wait for help to arrive. That's all there is to it.'

'You can stay,' said Samantha, standing up. 'I'm getting out of here.'

'Works for me,' said Lauren.

'If we make it, we'll tell everyone you're up here,' promised Jasmine.

'*Well*,' scoffed Josh, momentarily disconcerted, 'I should've guessed you people would have no qualms about leaving your schoolmates behind. It's everyone for themselves with you lot, isn't it? But, Ben,' he added, turning, 'I'd thought better of you. I thought perhaps that loyalty to your school might mean something more to you. Clearly I was wrong.'

'Josh,' said Robert firmly and exasperatedly, 'just *shut up*.'

Ben stared at him. Robert's days of crawling for Josh's favour were gone, it seemed. Stunned by this mutiny from the last of his supporters, Josh blinked several times then fell silent.

'All right,' said Samantha, turning to Ben. 'How're we going to do this?'

Ben made a face. 'It was my idea: I guess I ought to go first, just in case it turns out to be as stupid as Josh says. If I hit a dead end too soon, I'll turn around and come back. If I get anywhere useful, I'll try to signal you somehow. And if you don't hear from me and, er, I don't come back . . .'

'Good luck, Ben,' said Jasmine. 'We'll be waiting.'

'I don't suppose anyone's got something like a torch I could borrow, by any chance?' Ben asked.

Jasmine gave him a sympathetic look, but no one answered.

Ben pursed his lips. Fair enough: he didn't exactly tend to carry torches around with him at all times just in case, either. Well, there was nothing more to be said. The lockers squeaked ominously as he climbed back on top of them. He pushed out the square tile that was nearest to the thick bar in the ceiling. Then, after a lot of wriggling and struggling that he was certain would thoroughly undermine anything heroic about his exit, Ben climbed through the gap.

11:07 PM.

The bar in the ceiling was maybe twenty centimetres wide. Ben realized he was going to have to lie on his chest, using his arms and legs to push himself along through the darkness. His school shirt and trousers scraped along the surface of the bar with a gritty, grating sound. Before the receding light from the security room behind him got too faint, he stopped to look at his right hand: his pale skin was already charcoal-grey with the dust of decades. It was filthy up there. His eyes and nose itched abominably.

Ben pushed on. The dark around him deepened, and he began to imagine things.

He thought about the storey above: if he lifted himself off

the ceiling bar even a little he could feel it against his back –
concrete, rough and unforgiving. He imagined its solidity, its
weight. He imagined it sinking, the gap getting narrower until
he was trapped, squashed flat, or just stuck there for ever. Then
he imagined the contents of the darkness to either side of him
– armies of crawlers keeping silent pace with him, biding their
time, watching how far he'd get, while in the rooms below
ranks of enslaved adults waited, still as statues. Bolts, screws
and other protrusions from the bar kept stubbing his fingers
or scraping his belly, but Ben didn't mind. These things were
better than what was in his head.

Then – *whump* – his head hit something.

The ceiling cavity was so dark by now that he hadn't seen
anything coming. He flinched so violently he almost fell off the
bar, and had to hold on tight for a moment.

When he'd got himself together he reached forward with
his right hand. He felt bricks and mortar, blocking the way
ahead up to the ceiling and stretching away to either side.

Ben had crawled past three internal plasterboard walls
since the first one he'd left behind. The room beneath him
was therefore the fourth along the passage from the security
room. He had no idea how far he'd travelled in terms of actual
distance but he hoped it was enough to get a head-start on
the sentries. Because this, he realized, was as far along as he
or anyone else in the group was going to get.

Nervously he reached out with his left hand and scrabbled in the dust and fluff for the edge of the nearest ceiling tile. He found one, and dug at it with his fingertips until it lifted. Gently, silently, but fighting another sudden and terrible urge to sneeze, Ben laid the tile on the upper surface of one of its neighbours. Then he peered into the square of empty space it had left behind.

There was a thin line of light that Ben immediately identified as coming from the gap under a door. The light, presumably from the passageway outside, stopped at the edge of something that Ben realized could be close to his face. Heart pounding a bit, he reached through the gap and felt around with his hand. He was right: just below him was a long edge of something – a shelf, he realized.

Ben knew the room was small: he'd only just passed the last internal wall when he'd met the brick one. He craned his neck down to see if he could make out more details, and his dark-adapted eyes found the looming silhouettes of what could be more shelves.

He removed the ceiling tile that was just to the left of his knees, placing it somewhere off to his right, as before. Trying as best he could not to allow any of his body weight to press down anywhere else, he wriggled around until he was in position to feed his feet through the gap. He kept wriggling – lying crosswise on the bar now – until his legs, then his waist, could follow his feet into the room below. Of course he still couldn't reach the floor, even with the tips of his toes: he wasn't tall enough. He held the edge of the ceiling bar as tightly as he could, partly because as he pushed himself through the gap he was supporting more and more of his weight, but partly also because he knew that in a moment he would have to let the bar go. Once he did, there might be no way up again.

He let it go anyway.

Ben landed almost instantly, stumbling a little, but managed not to lose his balance. Turning to face the light under the door, he groped forward like a blind man until his hands met the door's sides, feeling around for a switch. He found one. When his eyes adjusted to the sudden glare of the overhead bulb, Ben looked around.

He was in a broom cupboard.

Three of the broom cupboard's walls were lined almost floor-to-ceiling with the shelves he had noticed before. The shelves were quite deep, and the room was so small that the ones to Ben's left and right almost met the sides of the door. There were perhaps two square metres of floor space – which, Ben supposed grudgingly, was actually quite big for a broom cupboard. But the place was still a broom cupboard, and not much to look at, particularly after the effort he'd made to get there.

Grimly, Ben started looking around for anything that might be . . . useful.

There was a vacuum cleaner, tucked in the gap under the lowest shelf, in the cupboard's left-hand corner from where Ben was standing. Yes, undoubtedly 'useful' for its purpose, but not quite what he had in mind.

The shelves were stacked with cleaning products – packets of dusters and bottles of chemicals. Ben had seen a film once in which the hero had mixed a few common household chemicals in various proportions and produced some handily powerful home-made explosives. Detailed instructions had not been provided.

There was a mop and bucket. The mop handle was made of wood, about a metre and a half long and quite solid-looking. Ben supposed that this, held quarterstaff-style, might make a useful mêleé weapon: a fabulous martial artist like Jackie Chan or Tony Jaa would have no trouble holding off a horde of bitten adults with that. But Ben was not a fabulous martial artist.

There was a toolbox. Ben opened it without much enthusiasm but was still disappointed to find that it only contained the things you usually find in a toolbox. Not even a crowbar. Just a hammer, a spirit level and an assorted bunch of ordinary screwdrivers. You might hurt someone (or something) with those, Ben supposed, but only if they were close enough to grab you already, and by then it would probably be too late.

Josh had been right. This room *was* worse than the security room. Ben's idea of finding an escape route for everyone, the idea that had caused Jasmine to smile at him in that wonderful way, had turned out to be nothing more than a waste of everyone's time. Alone, covered in dust, Ben stood in the broom cupboard and sighed.

Then Samantha stuck her head through the hole in the ceiling.

11:14 PM.

'Wow,' said Samantha. 'This is your way out?'

Ben watched as her eyes flicked around the broom cupboard, taking in the details.

She smirked. 'No offence or anything, but it's a bit crap, isn't it?'

'I thought,' said Ben, attempting to regain some control over the situation, 'that the idea was that everyone was going to wait for my signal. What are you doing here?'

'Fancied a change of scene,' said Samantha blithely. Then: 'Turn around.'

'Why?'

'Because I'm coming down, I'm in a skirt, and I don't want you eyeing up my knickers. Obviously.'

'Oh,' said Ben, colouring slightly. 'Right.' He turned to face the door. He heard scuffling, wriggling, the slap of feet meeting floor, then Samantha was in the broom cupboard with him.

'You can turn back now.'

When he did so, Samantha was smiling and looking him straight in the eye. Both legs of her black school tights were laddered, exposing bare, pale skin. Her white school blouse was smeared with dust and dirt from the ceiling cavity. Her face was grubby. Her blonde hair was tousled. As she stood there, hand on hip, Ben was uncomfortably aware that the broom cupboard, no palace to begin with, seemed to have halved in size.

'Look at this place,' said Samantha, still grinning. 'Lauren's going to freak. She's claustrophobic, remember?'

'Lauren's coming too?' asked Ben, horrified. 'What for?'

'Same reason as me,' said Samantha. 'Because we thought you'd found us a way out. Or were you maybe planning to ditch us all and go off by yourself, like your mate said?'

'Josh isn't my mate.'

'Is anyone?' asked Samantha, innocently.

Ben frowned at her. 'I was just about to climb back up,' he said. 'I was going tell everyone this was a dead end.'

'Whatever,' said Samantha, losing interest in him and looking instead at the surrounding shelves and their contents.

'Can't you go tell Lauren to go back?' he asked.

'She's probably halfway here by now. She'll have had a bad enough time just getting on the bar-thing. If I tell her to go back, she'll just freeze completely, then we'll be stuck here. In this cupboard.' Samantha smirked again. 'Just the two of us.'

Ben was starting to get infuriated. Samantha was so impossible, he found himself wanting to say something – anything – to take that smirk off her face.

'That stuff you said before,' he began. 'You don't seriously think Jasmine's got a crawler on her, do you?'

Samantha's eyes glittered. 'Why? D'you fancy her or something?'

'No,' said Ben. Then: 'Well, that's got nothing to do with it.'

Samantha raised an eyebrow.

'What I mean is,' said Ben quickly, 'was that stuff about Jasmine being a traitor just to wind her up, or what?'

Samantha's eyes narrowed. 'You don't know Jasmine,' she said. 'You never laid eyes on her before tonight.'

'That's true,' said Ben. 'But—'

'I'm at school with her,' said Samantha. 'I tell you, she's changed.'

Ben blinked. 'How do you mean?'

Before she answered, Samantha looked quickly up at the hole in the false ceiling. Then she took a step closer to Ben.

'I don't like her,' she said. 'That's no secret, you must have figured that out by now. But do you want to know why?'

'If you like.'

'She's *cold*,' said Samantha. She grimaced. 'Unfriendly. Her first day at Swatham I tried to get talking to her, we all did, but she blanked us. It's been the same ever since. Oh, in class she's always first with her hand up, always brown-nosing – but outside? Nothing.' Samantha sneered. 'Jasmine's too good for the rest of us. She's always kept herself to herself. Only now . . .' She frowned.

'What?' said Ben.

'Now she won't shut up! The whole night she's yapping – we should do this, we shouldn't do that. Worse than your mate Josh.'

'I told you,' said Ben, 'he's not my—'

'Listen,' said Samantha, stepping so close to Ben now that he could feel the warm breath that came with her words. 'Something's definitely different about Jasmine tonight. The way she speaks, the way she's been acting – she's not normally like this. So *watch her*, that's all I'm saying.'

Ben had heard almost the exact same words, he realized, from Jasmine herself. But he was distracted: over the last minute or so, while Samantha had been speaking, Ben had begun to hear a strange sound. It was a sort of low groaning, punctuated by moments of silence so regular that they seemed almost mechanical.

'*AWWW-huh-huh-hurr*,' it went. Then again: '*AWWW-huh-huh-hurr.*'

The sound was getting louder as it came closer. It was coming from the ceiling.

Lauren's face, when it appeared, was already a picture of misery. Tears and snot had left trails in the dirt on her cheeks. Her red eyes rolled in their sockets like those of a frightened horse. The journey through the ceiling cavity had obviously been rough on her. But then, as Samantha had warned, Lauren caught sight of her destination. Her lips puckered, trembled, then parted, releasing a high wail that set Ben's teeth on edge.

'Quiet!' he barked, in a desperate stage whisper. 'The adults are just down the passage!'

'Babes,' Samantha commanded.

'But it's smaller than the other place!' Lauren moaned. 'I *can't*!'

'Come on, babes. Come down with us, you'll be fine . . .' Samantha began to coax Lauren through the movements she would need to make to join them in the cupboard.

Cursing inwardly, Ben turned to face the door again.

'Where's Jasmine?' asked Samantha, once Lauren had dropped heavily to the floor.

'Right here,' said Jasmine – startling Ben again.

She slipped through the ceiling gap easily, landing neatly on both feet.

And now there were four of them in there.

11:19 PM.

Ben had two older sisters. Back when his family still went on holidays together he'd got used to spending long car journeys with them all crammed together on the back seat while their parents sat in relative comfort up front. Sharing a broom cupboard with three girls he barely knew, however, was a novel experience for him.

His brain started filling with unhelpful thoughts, mostly centred around the worry of touching someone inappropriately by accident – and exactly how mortifying that would be. Under the dust and grime his skin began to prickle. He found himself pressing his back against the door.

'Well isn't this cosy?' said Samantha, grinning in his face. 'Poor Jasmine and Ben,' she went on, looking from one to the other. 'You'd probably be all right if it was just the two of you in here. In fact,' she added, 'I think Ben here might even quite like it.'

Lauren stopped snivelling and cracked a smile. Ben flushed beetroot-red and found something to look at on the floor – not that he could see much of it with everyone standing in there. He didn't know what Jasmine's expression was, and didn't dare look at her to find out.

'Yeah, *whatever*, Samantha,' he heard Jasmine say. 'If you don't mind, some of us are trying to concentrate on how to get us out of here. Now: I counted three rooms that we passed on the way here. Is that right?'

'Yeah,' said Ben gruffly. 'That's right.'

'Well, do you think we've got far enough along the passage to get around the guards?'

'One way to find out,' said Samantha. Brushing against Ben's stomach with her arm, she reached past him for the doorknob.

'No! *Wait!*'

To everyone's relief, Samantha hesitated.

'We might only get one shot at this,' said Jasmine quickly, 'so let's do it carefully. Ben, did you find anything in here that might help us?'

Ben pulled himself together. 'I, um, didn't see anything that exactly jumped out at me,' he said. 'There are some bits and pieces in the toolbox. Otherwise the closest thing we've got to a weapon in here is probably that mop.' He gestured bleakly towards the corner where it stood.

'Then you should have that,' said Jasmine, twisting round with difficulty to reach it. Lauren was pressed up against her, but managed to pass it over.

Ben reached past Samantha, who was smiling again, and grasped the wooden shaft. It was reassuringly solid, and it did feel good in his hand, even if he didn't have much of an idea of what to do with it.

'Our hero,' quipped Samantha, in a sarcastic breathy voice.

Ben scowled and said nothing.

'Anyone want anything from the toolbox?' asked Jasmine. 'Lauren, you can take this hammer. Me and Samantha'll go with these screwdrivers. Better than nothing.'

Lauren looked at the hammer in her hand, nonplussed, as if she'd never seen one before.

'All right,' said Jasmine. '*Now* I guess we open the door.'

'Hold on,' said Ben. 'I've got to say it: what if we *haven't* gone far enough? I mean, to be honest, before you three got here I was kind of all set to come back and tell everyone this place was a dead end.'

'You think we should go back?' asked Jasmine seriously.

'Well . . . yeah,' said Ben. He shrugged. 'Maybe. I don't know.'

Lauren's knuckles whitened on the black rubber of the hammer's grip. She sniffed again, but resolutely this time. 'I ain't going back,' she said.

'Me neither,' said Samantha, who had finally stopped grinning. 'I've had enough of that room, whatever happens to us out here.'

'Ben?' said Jasmine.

He blinked. 'All right,' he said.

'All right,' echoed Jasmine with a quick, tight smile. 'We take our chances. Everyone ready?'

No one replied.

Ben turned to face the door for the last time. He put his hand on the doorknob, visions of Hugo's last moments in the security room flashing through his mind. He took a deep breath, hefted his mop in his left hand, turned the knob gently, and pulled.

Directly outside the door, the passage was empty. He saw grey concrete walls and shiny, red, brick-shaped floor tiles that glittered faintly under the strip lights above.

Holding his breath, he peered out.

There they were – the sentries, standing frozen outside the security-room door, some twenty metres away. There were fewer of them than Ben had been expecting. They were turned inward around the door, still concentrating on that. They had their backs to him. And one of them was Hugo.

He was standing there like a statue, just like the others. Ben could see the crawler on the back of his neck.

Ben gulped. But his plan had worked. They had a chance.

'What can you see?' hissed Samantha in his ear, making Ben almost jump out of his skin. Infuriated, he turned and put his finger to his lips, but Samantha just raised her eyebrows and turned her palms up in a *Well?* gesture.

Before he spoke Ben glanced out into the passage again, taking a second to get the details straight in his head.

'We could make it to the lifts,' he mouthed, still not daring to breathe. 'But we obviously can't just press a button and then stand there waiting for one to arrive: the sentries would get us. I think we'll have to try for the stairs.'

'What?' Samantha whispered back, cupping a hand around her ear.

'I said,' Ben hissed, 'I think we'll have to try for the stairs.'

The glass-sided stairwell was just a little further along the passage than the lifts, which were just a few metres away. The double doors that gave access to the stairs were that much closer to the sentries, but Ben figured that way lay their only chance. He supposed they would just have to tiptoe out, and hope they weren't heard. It was a desperate plan, but it was all he'd got.

'Eh?' said Lauren. 'I can't hear you. What did you say?'

'Heaven's sake,' said Ben, losing patience. 'I . . .' By chance, before repeating himself a second time he decided to risk a quick glance at the sentries.

It was lucky he did. They had just started to turn towards him.

'Oh crap,' he said. 'Run!'

11:21 pm.

Clutching his mop, Ben launched himself out of the door just as, with the same eerie synchronicity that characterized all their movements, the sentries spun round to face him.

Ben sprinted up the corridor, the soles of his school shoes slapping on the brick-shaped tiles, his heart pounding loud in his ears. He reached the double doors to the stairs just when the sentries opened their mouths and started screaming.

He skidded to a halt, frozen in his tracks as much by the sound as by the fact he'd reached his goal. The crowd by the security-room door had obviously thinned out at some point over the course of the evening: while there had been nearly thirty people visible on the monitors earlier, now there were 'only' ten, plus Hugo. (*Where are all the others?* wondered a part of Ben's mind dazedly.) At any rate, the remaining group, a roughly even mix of men and women, certainly made a thoroughly bloodcurdling noise.

They just stood there at first, their voices rising like sirens until each of them found the highest, most piercing note they could reach, then they held it. Heads trembled. Chins wobbled. Staring eyes threatened to pop out of sockets. Hugo was right there screaming with them. Their hands lifted from their sides. Then, still screaming, they charged.

As he watched them come Ben's thoughts ran something like this:

He had to hold them off until Jasmine, Samantha and Lauren were through the doors. He had to do this because he had the mop. Ben was no martial artist, but if he held the stick crosswise, just above waist height, he might temporarily be able to stop the sentries from getting past him, giving the girls the crucial seconds they needed to catch up, get the doors open and get through. It wasn't the most sophisticated plan in the world: it was expediency, pure and simple, with no thought for anything beyond the next few moments. But, as before, it was all he had.

He grasped his mop in both hands and tensed his arms out in front of him. Then Hugo barrelled into him.

Ben's legs were braced for the first impact but he didn't stand a chance. As three, four, five adults joined forces with Hugo against the mop handle the soles of Ben's shoes lost their grip, and now he was staggering backwards.

Ben's vision was a mass of snarling mouths. Suddenly something grabbed at his back and waist and pulled him sideways. He swung round helplessly, struggling to keep his feet, and—

Crack!

The ends of the mop met the doorway to either side of him.

The last second or two had been so fast, Ben had lost track of what was going on. It seemed he was now standing just inside the double doors, still facing outwards. And the girls were behind him.

'We need the stick!' someone yelled, right next to his ear. '*Push!*'

Ben felt hands shove at his back. He wasn't ready. He fell forward, his elbows bent and he met the hard wooden pole with his unprotected ribs. But he kept his footing, tensed his legs and shoved, adding his strength to that of whoever was pushing him. To his astonishment it actually worked. Taken by surprise, Hugo and the adults fell back for a moment, but it was enough. The pole twisted Ben's wrists, came free from the doorway, was snatched from his hands. Then, while Ben fell back, Jasmine and Lauren slammed the doors shut and Samantha jammed the pole through the handles.

Crunch. The doors opened less than five centimetres, then stopped. For a moment Hugo's face smeared against the shatterproof glass, grimacing in frustration.

To Ben's amazement, the humble mop-stick had saved the day: it had held off the sentries and now it was barring the doors.

Hugo and the adults stood back, allowing the doors to swing fully closed again. Hugo's eyes locked onto Ben's, unblinking.

Ben's ribs were sore from where they'd made contact with

the pole. He stepped back and leaned against a railing to catch his breath. A big part of him didn't seem to want to take his eyes off Hugo, but he tore his gaze away to look at Jasmine, Lauren and Samantha. The girls must have already dropped the hammer and screwdrivers because now they were empty-handed, and breathing as hard as he was.

'We . . . did it,' he managed, more in surprise than triumph.

'Think . . . that'll hold them?' gasped Jasmine, pointing at the mop handle.

'Sure,' answered Hugo from the other side of the glass. 'For a while.'

As Ben and the three girls turned to stare at him again, Hugo smiled.

'You still don't get it, do you?' he said. 'We're not zombies. And nothing's "eating our brains".' He made little quote marks with his fingers around his own words from earlier.

Ben felt his skin crawl.

Still smiling, Hugo said: 'The Queen wants you to know she's impressed. But you won't get far. In fact you might as well give up right now.'

'And if we don't,' said Samantha, 'what are you going to do about it?'

Hugo's smile vanished. As one, he and the adults piled against the doors in a brutal shoulder-charge. *Crunch.* Black metal door handles bit into dark wood. The sentries reared back for another assault; released from their pressure the mop turned, exposing white splinter-marks.

But Ben, Jasmine, Lauren and Samantha had not hung around to see. They were already running downstairs.

'They made it!' said Robert, grinning delightedly at Josh.

The two boys were standing in the monitor room. After a lot of fiddling and tinkering with the console they had at last managed to find the view of the corridor again in time to witness the escape.

Robert was ecstatic. 'They did it! They really did it!' he said. Then he noticed Josh's expression. 'What?'

In answer, Josh just pointed numbly at another of the screens. This one was currently showing the Barbican foyer – and what was going on there.

'Oh,' said Robert. 'Oh, *no* . . .'

11:23 PM.

The stairs were encased in a sort of giant glass tube, ribbed with black metal struts and built into the side of the building. Through the glass, above the artificial pond and empty courtyard café outside, Ben could see a patch of open night sky.

Like all night skies in London it was stained yellowish-purple with light pollution. It was hemmed in by buildings: skyscrapers jabbed up into it like pointing black fingers, but the moon was bright. This was the first time Ben had seen outside the Barbican for a while, and the effect the sight had on him was surprisingly strong. Maybe he was just high on adrenaline, but as he ran down the grey-carpeted stairs after the girls it seemed like they had a chance. They were on their way! *They might actually get out of there!* Then he turned a corner, saw the doors to the next floor, and stopped.

1: HALL BALCONY, said the sign by the glass doors, but what Ben was seeing didn't seem to make any sense. He could see the balcony – a carpeted walkway, open from waist height on one side, heading out from the doors at an angle to the left – but it was obscured by some sort of mist. Beyond the balcony, where he expected to see the foyer's lights, its giant concrete walls, the open space of the room itself, there was nothing but a bank of stained whiteness – a thick fog of some kind. Wisps of it were drifting through the gaps around the doors, out into the landing. As Ben stood there his nose twitched, his eyes prickled and he began to register something harsh and strange about the air he was breathing.

'What is this, now?' he asked.

'It's gas,' said Jasmine, as if she hardly believed it.

'Gas don't smell like that,' said Lauren firmly.

'Not the kind in pipes at home,' said Jasmine patiently.

'I think it's tear gas.' She looked at Ben. 'Maybe the police are about to have another go at storming the building.'

'What are you on about?' said Samantha.

'We saw it on the monitors, remember?' said Jasmine. 'The police keep trying to get in, but the bitten people and the crawlers keep catching them. Maybe now they've decided to get serious.'

'But . . . *we're* in here,' whined Lauren. 'What about us?'

'What *about* us?' said Ben bleakly.

'No one outside knows anything about us,' said Jasmine. 'We've got no way to contact them. And after what's happened whenever they've tried to get in so far, I bet they'll be assuming that everyone in the building has been bitten. Us included.'

'Maybe they're not completely wrong,' said Samantha, looking hard at Jasmine.

'But *we're in here*,' Lauren repeated, louder, dismissing what she obviously saw as side issues to her main point. '*How are we going to get out?*'

'Sshhh,' said Jasmine. 'Hold on a second. Just listen.'

Ben waited, holding his breath. All he could hear was the distant rhythm of Hugo and the sentries upstairs still trying to get through the doors. *Crunch. CRUNCH.*

'I don't know how much longer that mop handle's going to hold,' said Samantha, voicing Ben's thoughts.

'Shh!' Jasmine repeated, annoyed.

'What?' snapped Samantha. 'I can't hear anything else! Can you?'

'No,' said Jasmine grimly. 'I can't. And that means now's the best time.'

'For what?' said Ben.

'For us to go out there,' said Jasmine. 'Now, before anything else happens. It might be our only chance.'

With that, she stripped off her school tie, undid its knot, and began bundling it up in her hands.

'The main entrance is on the other side of the foyer,' she explained, nodding at the fog beyond the balcony railing. 'That's where the police keep trying to get in, so that's got to be the closest place we can find people to help us. All we've got to do is get there.'

'Oh no,' said Samantha, noticing what Jasmine was doing with her tie. 'Oh, you've got to be kidding!'

'We breathe through these,' said Jasmine, holding the bundled material up to her nose and mouth. 'It's going to be horrible, but it's all we've got.'

The girls' school ties were thicker than Ben's – more like short scarves, really. The extra width of their material meant that, folded, a good two or three layers could be held over both nose and mouth at the same time.

Ben's tie, by contrast, was narrow – an ungenerous six

centimetres across even at its widest point. No matter how he scrunched its rough red polyester to his face, it felt alarmingly loose and useless – nothing like airtight. He grimaced.

The expression was only for himself, but Samantha caught his eye and gave him a significant look. Ben deliberately didn't react, just looked at Jasmine.

Samantha's wrong, he told himself. Jasmine couldn't possibly have a crawler on her – could she? But her apparent utter certainty about what their next step should be did suddenly seem a bit weird.

'I . . . don't know,' he said. 'Do you think we maybe ought to see if there's another way out first?'

Jasmine frowned. For a second Ben thought she looked disappointed in him – which, he realized, was something he didn't like one bit.

'They locked us in, Ben,' she said. 'Remember? The staff shut all the doors when this thing started. We might search the whole building and never find a way out – assuming, of course, that we don't get caught in the meantime. But this . . .' She gestured at the fog again. 'This is close! From the doors below us, it's just a straight run across the foyer. We've got to take the chance.'

Lauren looked to her mistress for guidance. 'Babes?'

'Well . . . OK,' said Samantha. 'But if this gas is poisonous or something, you're in *so* much trouble, Jasmine.'

'We'll all be,' said Ben. He shrugged and shook his head. 'All right.'

They turned to set off down the stairs again – and two things happened at once.

There was a splintering *crack*, a crash of doors thrown back on their hinges, and a terrible discordant shriek as eleven voices rose in triumph. On the floor above, Hugo and the adults had broken through.

The second thing was that Ben, Jasmine, Samantha and Lauren caught sight of another group of adults who had been sneaking up the stairs behind them, from below.

Their approach had been silent. They had already reached the half-landing between the floors, just six steps down. If Ben and the girls had turned just seconds later they would have had no chance. As it was, a precious chunk of what little warning they got was wasted on Ben, because all he could do was stand and gape.

The adults stood four abreast, their formation snaking round the curve of the stairs and out of sight. In the front row, mouth opening in a wide grin of triumph, was Ben's tutor, Mr Clissold.

'Follow me!' yelled Jasmine. She clamped her tie to her face, yanked the balcony door open and set off into the fog at a run. Lauren followed her, then Samantha.

For another slow second Ben watched in horror as Mr

Clissold abandoned stealth and sprang up the stairs, hands poised to grab him. At last Ben turned, the sign by the door saying 1: HALL BALCONY blurring in his vision. Then, holding his school tie over his mouth, he plunged out into the mist.

11:25 PM.

It was like someone had dashed acid in Jasmine's face. Her visibility, fogged to start with, instantly dropped almost to zero as her eyes wept furiously to protect themselves. Though she was pressing her school tie to her mouth and nose with both hands, the gas still sent what felt like sparks to the back of her throat, scorching down into her lungs. But she kept running.

It was impossible to tell exactly how many pairs of feet were pounding the Barbican carpet behind her – it sounded like a lot of them. She hoped Samantha and Lauren and Ben were still with her (*If anyone got caught*, she told herself, *they would have made a noise – wouldn't they?*) But even if they were, they definitely weren't alone. The multiple clumps of closing footsteps were the only sounds Jasmine could hear.

Her heart juddered in her chest; panic jangled in her mind. The way those adults had snuck up on them was like something out of a nightmare. The silence now also grated at her nerves: Jasmine would have preferred shouts and noise, even the screams that had come from Hugo and the sentries, but there was nothing but footsteps.

Ahead of her in the mist and a little off to the left, a row of yellow lights appeared. The lights had black markings that resolved themselves into stick figures, male and female. Jasmine had just identified them as toilet signs when the grey concrete wall they were attached to abruptly loomed out behind them, forcing Jasmine to swerve left. The pursuing footsteps followed her, getting closer.

Jasmine hoped it was Ben and Samantha and Lauren back there, but she was so scared it wasn't, she didn't dare look round to find out.

As she ran, she tried to keep the position of the main entrance and her relationship to it anchored in her mind. By setting out at an angle from the doors, the balcony walkway had taken her off at a tangent, and this wall Jasmine was following had turned her even further. At some point, she hoped, there would be another way down to the foyer: if there wasn't, she was taking Ben, Samantha and Lauren into a dead end. But if she *did* find a way down, she would then have to find her way back to the main entrance from wherever she'd ended up – and the Barbican was hard enough to navigate even when it *wasn't* filled with tear gas and enemies.

She needn't have worried about finding the stairs, at least: to Jasmine's horror, with her next step her left foot dropped further than she'd expected. She lurched forward, barely keeping her balance, feet clattering, pain jarring through her ankles and knees. But the flight was mercifully short: twelve steps later she was on flat floor again. As footsteps thundered down the stairs behind her Jasmine took a chance. She pulled the tie from her mouth, yelled *'Left!'* and swerved again, hard.

Instantly one of the foyer's giant concrete pillars seemed to lunge at her out of the thickening fog. Jasmine managed not to run straight into it: instead she used it to orient herself, running around it. She was now moving parallel with the wall she'd followed earlier past the toilets. Now, however, she was one floor down, and running in the opposite direction – or so she hoped.

Jasmine was now on the foyer's upper level – where the main entrance was. She was conscious of the space opening out around her but the gas was thicker down here: it seemed to claw at her eyes. Denied the senses of sight and smell she concentrated on sound, but what she heard was strange and frightening. Gasps and hisses came out of the fog all around her. She heard sudden movements: their origins and direction were impossible to identify, but her heart was gripped with a sudden, icy certainty that there were living things in the mist with her, reacting to her, aware of where she was. At any second, she was sure, someone or something was about to leap out and grab her. But still the pursuing footsteps continued to pound at her heels, driving her on.

Was she going the right way? Were the others even still with her?

11:27 PM.

Acid ate his lungs; his eyes felt like they were melting – but Ben was keeping up. With both hands pressing his tie to his face he had made it down the stairs without breaking his legs. He had followed Jasmine's voice around the corner without smacking into the concrete pillar. He had kept Samantha or Lauren's back in sight (the fog was so thick and his eyes so raw, he couldn't tell which of them it was), and so far – though there had been a nasty moment near the start of the chase when he had felt fingertips actually touch the back of his shirt – he had managed to avoid being caught. But then his left foot got tangled round the leg of some piece of furniture.

Ben spun. His right knee buckled painfully as his weight hit it at the unexpected angle. Then he was on the floor.

His breath flew out in a rush. Black spots burst in his vision against the surrounding yellow-white of the fog. He lay there, winded, utterly helpless, certain that his pursuers were about to get him.

Nothing happened.

Hands still at his sides, Ben snatched a breath. Mistake. The tie had been an intolerable hindrance, but the price of trying to breathe without it was one he paid in pain: it felt like his insides were being scoured out with bleach. He hawked and wheezed, rolling on the carpet, still expecting hands (or worse) to descend on him at any moment. *Where are they?* he thought dazedly. Why hadn't they caught him? What was going on?

Ben brought the tie back to his mouth and gradually brought his breathing under some sort of control. As he did so he noticed that, apart from the noise he himself was making, the room around him seemed to have become unnervingly silent.

Slowly, carefully, aching, he got to his feet.

Was it really the police who had released the gas, like Jasmine had said? If so, Ben wasn't sure what good it was supposed to do. Maybe it had stopped the bitten people, maybe not. But for him it was a nightmare.

There was no way to tell which way he was facing. Deciding that whichever way it was would have to do, he shuffled forward. With one hand he kept the tie over his nose and mouth. With the other he stretched out, eyes streaming, blindly groping at the air ahead of him.

After ten slow paces his right foot came to the edge of a drop: he realized it was the top of another flight of stairs.

Ben concentrated, trying to visualize what he remembered of the foyer's layout. He shuffled to his left, following the line of the stair, and decided that there were two possibilities. He was either on the central walkway of the foyer, which would be absolutely amazing, because it would mean he was now perhaps twenty metres or so from the main entrance. Or, of course, he was completely lost, in which case he was just stuffed.

Where were the girls? Had they gone on ahead? Why was everything so quiet all of a sudden? Ben took his tie from his mouth.

'Jasmine?' he croaked. 'Samantha? Lauren?' Then he waited, uncomfortably aware that he had just given away his position in the fog to anyone else who might be able to hear him.

'Ben?'

His heart jumped. 'Jasmine?'

'Ben? Are you OK?'

'I'm fine!' said Ben, absurdly relieved. 'Where are you?'

Three figures holding ties over their faces materialized around him.

'I heard you fall,' said Jasmine. 'Are you OK?'

'Tripped,' said Ben. 'A real face-plant. But they didn't get me.'

'That's what you'd say if they *did* get you,' said Samantha.

'What?' she added, when everyone looked at her. 'We lost sight of him. Anything could've happened.'

'I . . . don't know why it didn't,' said Ben frankly. 'They were right behind me, but then they just . . . stopped.'

'Whatever,' said Samantha. 'Jasmine, now we've waited for your *boyfriend*, can we please get out of here?'

Ben looked at Jasmine. It was true, then: leaving aside Samantha's crack about his being her 'boyfriend' for a moment, Jasmine *had* come back for him. He felt a blaze of warmth towards her that, for a moment, made him forget their surroundings. Then:

'Get down on the floor!' shouted a voice from the whiteness up ahead. *'Get down now or we open fire!'*

The voice was strange – muffled-sounding, with a rasping, robotic edge to it. For a couple of seconds Ben and the girls just stood there, looking in the direction the voice had come from.

BADABLAM!

Ben had never heard gunfire in real life before, let alone at close range, but the numbing, dazzling, brutal effect of the sound provoked an immediate and instinctive reaction. He dropped flat on his face before he was even conscious of moving.

'Get down on the floor and stay down or we WILL shoot you!' roared the robotic voice.

Very, *very* slowly, Ben lifted his eyes from his second close-up view of the Barbican's carpet. The girls, like him, had obeyed the voice's instructions. To his left, Lauren was muttering hysterically: 'Oh Jesus, oh Jesus, oh Jesus . . .'

'Don't shoot!' shouted Jasmine. 'Don't shoot! Help us! We're . . . just . . . kids!' She had taken her tie off her mouth for extra volume, so this was as far as she got before being overcome by racking coughs.

There was a long pause.

'Stay face down on the ground,' said the robot voice. 'Keep your hands where we can see them: if you move, we shoot. We're coming to meet you now.'

Ben waited, his school tie still pressed firmly to his face. There was no way he was going to take his hands away – his lungs were hurting badly enough already.

He began to see movement in the fog – little flashing lines of something red and fast-moving. For a second he wondered whether this was some trick his eyes were playing due to the prolonged lack of clean air to breathe, but the lines came closer. They scythed through the fog. A red dot slithered across the Barbican carpet at the edge of Ben's peripheral vision. Then he realized what the lines were. They came from laser sights.

Shadows loomed out of the mist ahead.

The emerging figures were dressed in grey all-in-one protection suits. While they did have a slightly puffy appearance, the figures inside them seemed to move rapidly and easily. They all had guns. The guns were pointed at him and the girls. But what Ben found most frightening in what was already a pretty frightening situation was the figures' faces.

Instead of mouths they had neat, round cylinders. Instead of eyes, they had two black metal stalks, like snail-horns protruding from the front of their heads. *Gas masks and goggles*, Ben told himself consolingly. *That's all they are: gas masks and goggles.* But his brain didn't seem to want to listen. None of the bitten adults had guns (or not as far as he knew) so Ben supposed these people were meant to be rescuing them at last. After everything he and the others had been through, he should have been pleased to see them – but he wasn't. To Ben the figures looked as alien and monstrous and horrifying as anything else he'd seen that night.

'Put your hands where I can see them,' rasped the nearest figure. '*Hands*,' it repeated, lifting its gun and taking aim at Ben's head, just as he realized belatedly that it was talking to him. '*Now!*'

Ben released his tie. He put his hands out flat on the carpeted floor, closed his eyes, and tried not to breathe.

'Who are you?' the voice grated. 'What's your name? Answer me!'

Ben heard a ratcheting click. 'Please!' he gasped. 'Don't shoot! I'm B-Ben. This is Samantha, and Jasmine, and Lauren. There are more of us trapped upstairs. We were here on a school trip. We need help. You have to let us out!'

It was desperately frustrating not being able to explain things any better, but now the urge to cough had claimed him too.

'What do you think, Sarge?' said the robot voice, as Ben hacked and spluttered.

Ben opened his eyes – and stared at the red laser dot on the carpet just centimetres from his face. The grey-suited figure had lowered his aim a little while waiting for his superior to answer, but his black snail-horn eyes had not stopped looking at Ben. The gun in his hands was still up and ready to fire. The slightest flick would plant that dot back on Ben's head, for death to follow it.

'Help us,' Ben heard Jasmine croak into the silence. 'You've got to help us!'

'. . . All right,' said the voice at last.

The figure put his gun down to his side, on its strap. Bending stiffly to one knee, it held out its black gloved hands.

'Come on,' it said. 'Come to me. You're coming with us.'

'Oh thank you,' blurted Lauren. 'Oh thank you, thank you, thank you!'

Ben too was so relieved and happy that, oddly, he had a sudden urge to laugh. Eyes streaming, lungs raw, grinning like an idiot, he wriggled onto all fours and retrieved his tie, pressing it back up against his face before preparing to follow the grey-suited figures to freedom.

That was when he heard the sound.

It was quiet at first, like the hiss of air escaping. But Ben knew what the sound really was even before it grew louder: it was screaming. A thousand voices, screaming.

Their pursuers had not given up on them. They had been lying in wait, using Ben and the girls as bait to lure the soldiers – more recruits to swell their numbers.

'*Ambush!*' roared robot-voice, coming to his feet again and bringing his gun to bear all in one fluid movement. 'Rawson to all units: it's a trap! These kids are just another *trap*!'

11:31 PM.

No, thought Ben. *No, no, NO*—! He dropped flat: his face greeted the Barbican carpet a third time. His consciousness, his whole being, was focused on the red laser dot that right then must have been settling, fatally, on the back of his skull.

The soldiers thought they'd been tricked: *they thought that he and the girls were part of it!* To die now, by mistake, so close to getting help – not just for the four of them but for Robert, Josh and Lisa too – it just didn't seem fair. Now the soldiers would see them as a threat. The nearest figure's finger would be tightening on the trigger. Ben squeezed his eyes shut, awaiting annihilation. But at the same time the screams of the charging horde were getting closer. He heard the drumming of approaching feet. *They were right behind him—*

And now they attacked.

Abandoning his school tie, Ben threw his hands up over his head and drew in his legs until he was a ball: he wanted to be smaller; he wanted to make himself disappear as hundreds of pounding feet stormed past, threatening to trample him. Gunfire; screaming; choking smoke; thundering footsteps; roaring voices – it all came to Ben in flashes. He could make sense of none of it. He just wanted it to end.

Eventually the trampling feet passed. Now someone was shaking him. He flinched and slapped the hands away. Then he opened his eyes.

Jasmine was crouching over him. 'Come on, Ben!' she shouted. 'Get up! Quick, while they're fighting by the doors!'

As he got to his knees Ben turned to look. He couldn't help himself.

The noise and movement of the battle had dispersed some of the gas. Ben could see a little of what was going on. In the background he saw the main body of the horde of parasitized adults. From where he was standing they were a row of backs swarming against the doors of the main entrance, hurling and battering themselves at the glass. Obviously there was no way out there. But at that moment Ben's attention was mostly on what was happening in the foreground, only a few metres away.

Four adults were bent over, wrestling with something on the ground. Catching a flash of grey movement between them, Ben stared: one of the men in protection suits – possibly Rawson himself – was down, and struggling furiously. As Ben watched, the attackers were just getting the upper hand: while a fat red-faced man in a pinstriped suit immobilized their victim's legs by sitting on them, two snarling old ladies trapped his arms. The fourth member of the group, a young woman in a smart grey jacket and matching trousers, pulled a crawler from her handbag. With her free hand she ripped off her victim's hood, mask and goggles, then brought the eager, grasping creature down on the back of the man's head.

The young woman was the girls' teacher, Ms Gresham.

Ben gulped and looked quickly back at Jasmine, deciding not to tell her. 'Wh-what about the others?' he asked instead.

'Lauren ran off,' said Jasmine. 'Samantha went after her. We've got to follow them, quick, or we'll get separated.' She tugged on his arm again. *'Ben!'*

'Right,' he said. 'Right. Yes.' Everything was happening so fast, his brain was having trouble keeping up. He retrieved his school tie and got to his feet. 'Um, which way did they go?'

Jasmine held out a hand. 'Come on!'

To Ben's right lay the stairs he'd found earlier. Jasmine took them two at a time. It was a short flight leading down to a small mezzanine floor from which more stairs led off to the left, these ones flanked by concrete pillars.

Hold on, thought Ben as he passed the pillars and reached the bottom. He'd been this way before . . .

'Let me out!' wailed a familiar voice from Ben's left. 'I've got to get out of here! *LET ME OUT!'*

At least Lauren hadn't proved too hard to find: when Jasmine and Ben reached her, she was pounding on one of the glass panel exit doors which, from this level, led out towards the Barbican's underground car park. Neither Lauren's pounding nor her yelling was doing the least bit of good: the doors had been locked for nearly four hours now. But Samantha's efforts to stop her were proving just as fruitless.

'Babes, you've got to calm down.'

'No! I've had it! I can't take this any more! *Let me out!'*

'Please be quiet,' said Ben hopelessly. 'We don't know if we're alone down here.'

'We should get out of sight,' agreed Jasmine. 'At least until this fighting stops. Is there – I don't know – maybe somewhere we can hide and get our breath back, work out our next move?'

'Oh, sure,' said Samantha, rounding on her, 'because everything turned out *so* well the last time you had that idea.'

'Well what do *you* suggest, Samantha?' Jasmine snapped back.

'We could try the theatre,' said Ben. He pointed at another set of double doors off to their left. 'It's just through there.'

The doors he was indicating were the same ones he'd used at the start of the evening. They led to the stalls of the Barbican's Main Theatre, where his tutor group's seats had been for the play.

All three girls looked at him – even, Ben was surprised to notice, Lauren.

'But it's *dark*,' she said indignantly, frowning at him.

Lauren's point might be random but it was also true: beyond the glass panels, the blackness was total. Still, Ben couldn't help wondering whether the boys of the group would also have picked this minute to have an argument.

BLAM! BADABLAM! More shots momentarily drowned out the screams upstairs.

'At least we won't be in the middle of a battle,' Ben pointed out.

11:34 PM.

The glass doors were designed to be soundproof: the noise of the fight in the Barbican foyer was cut off as they closed, plunging the four of them into silence. In the limited light that came through from the foyer behind them, Jasmine looked at the others.

Ben's, Samantha's and Lauren's reddened eyes were wide, and they were all breathing hard – gulping greedily at what was the closest to clean air they'd had to breathe in what had felt like for ever. *Wide eyes; fast breathing*, Jasmine thought: classic panic symptoms. But she was starting to feel something else. The night's pattern of constant, gnawing dread interspersed with blind terror had pushed Jasmine beyond basic fear now, into strange new territory. She felt a kind of hyper-awareness, dreamlike but intense. She was walking an emotional knife-edge from which she could fall in any direction: part of her felt like screaming or crying, sure, but another part worryingly felt like . . . laughing. It was exhausting, but also weirdly, dangerously exhilarating.

Samantha was fiddling with her phone again.

'Got a signal yet?' asked Ben.

'No, but I have got this.' She showed him the phone's screen. She had turned on the backlight: the screen was lit up white, as bright as she could get it. 'It's not a torch, but . . .'

'That's good thinking,' said Jasmine.

Samantha sniffed. 'Don't sound so surprised.'

'Why didn't you think of this before?' asked Ben. 'I could've used that getting out of the security room.'

'What?' Samantha snorted. 'I was supposed to give you my *phone*?' She waited while Lauren tinkered with hers. Once that was lit too, she said: 'OK. Everyone follow me.'

There was a short carpeted landing, then a flight of wide steps that curved gently to the left. At the end of each of those steps, touched by the dim glow of the phones, was a row of empty seats.

Someone must have turned the lights off after the evacuation: deserted and dark, the theatre auditorium was very different to how Ben remembered it from the start of the evening. In the dark he felt the emptiness, like the silence, seem to swell around him – as if the room was alive, breathing. The theatre was much warmer than he remembered too, almost like a hothouse.

Why's there nobody here? Ben wondered. Of course it was a relief not being attacked or chased, but he felt an immediate and definite sense that coming into the theatre might have been a mistake.

The steps finished almost at the stage itself. 'All right!' said Samantha, immediately scrambling up onto it. 'Check me out!' She turned to face the darkness, and bowed. 'Thank you!' she said, acknowledging thunderous imaginary applause. 'You've been a beautiful audience! I love you all! Goodnight! God bless!'

There, thought Jasmine, gaping at her in astonishment.

That's why Samantha's the way she is. Her mind flashed to the conversation on the bus, all the way back at the start of the evening: like Jasmine, Samantha hadn't answered Ms Gresham's question about what she wanted to be. But unlike Jasmine, who simply didn't like talking about her plans in front of others, Samantha hadn't answered because she'd presumed it was obvious: she wanted to be famous. Even in the middle of everything that was happening, Samantha lived her whole life like it was a performance. And she couldn't stand to be ignored.

'You're a *star*, babes,' said Lauren, standing at Samantha's feet. 'The world may not know it yet, but you're going to be a real celebrity, I'm telling you.'

Her face lit eerily from below by her phone, Samantha smiled.

'What's that?' asked Ben, pointing.

'What's what?' said Samantha, annoyed that Ben had spoiled her moment.

At the back of the stage something had caught his eye. The light of Samantha's phone didn't travel far, but its glow had passed over several strange, pale shapes that loomed out of the darkness behind her.

Ben climbed up onto the stage and pointed again. 'Back there. I saw something that wasn't there before. Something . . . weird.'

Jasmine and Lauren clambered up to join him and Samantha. The four of them looked at each other in the phone-light.

'Should we check it out?' asked Ben.

'Do we have to?' asked Lauren.

'Stay here if you want,' said Jasmine. 'We won't go far.'

The production design for the play had been sparse and minimal, with no onstage furniture or props other than what the actors brought on with them: the stage was an empty space except for its backdrop, which was a large, wide expanse of plain, dark wood panelling that seemed to stretch up all the way to the Main Theatre's two-storey-high ceiling. But the backdrop wasn't plain or dark any more.

Some odd-looking, long, white objects had been stuck upright in rows against the wood. They were all of a similar size – around two metres tall and just less than a metre wide, rounded at the top and bottom. There were perhaps twenty of them in the row at stage level, and another twenty above that. But as Ben approached and the light from the girls' phones got stronger, he saw that there were twenty more above those, then *another* twenty, and so on, carrying on upwards further than the light could reach.

The white objects were bulbous and lumpish, and made of some opaque, resinous substance. The texture on the nearest was rope-like, yet also somehow dribbly or melted-looking. Its uneven surface twinkled stickily.

Samantha grimaced. 'Well, Professor?' she said, cocking her head at Jasmine. 'Got another theory to dazzle us all?'

'How should *I* know what these are?' asked Jasmine, annoyed. She considered the objects and frowned. 'They look a bit like . . . pupal casings, maybe.'

'Huh?'

'You know – cocoons? Like for caterpillars?'

Samantha snorted and grinned. 'Bit big for caterpillars, don't you think?'

Ben didn't see what she was grinning about: he didn't think this was funny. Besides, he had just noticed something else:

'This one's got shoes.'

It was true. In the second row up, a little higher than his eyeline, the toes of a large pair of battered-looking workman's boots were protruding from the front of the lower end of one of the cocoons. And once Ben saw the first pair, he started seeing shoes all over the wall – brogues, trainers, all sorts. He even spotted a section of smaller cocoons, high up, all sporting footwear similar to his own school shoes.

Ben took a step back. The bad feeling he'd had since they'd entered the theatre was intensifying.

'They've got *people* inside,' he murmured, feeling a sickly stirring in his stomach.

'Guys?' called Lauren suddenly. '*Guys!*'

Exchanging a startled look, the three of them went back to rejoin her.

'There's something in here with us,' hissed Lauren in a panicky whisper. She pointed at the empty auditorium. 'Out there.'

Everyone squinted into the darkness and held their breath.

'There's nothing,' said Jasmine.

Clunk.

'There!' said Lauren.

'I think one of the seats just moved,' Ben whispered. They were the kind that flip up when no one is sitting on them.

CLUNK, clunk.

Ben saw it that time: the second, softer *clunk* was an upholstered seat bouncing against its back. *Something was under the seats*. And it was getting closer.

'Is it the crawlers again?' asked Lauren.

'Can't be,' said Ben. 'They're too small.'

'Well, let's not wait here for it to attack us, whatever it is,' said Jasmine. Then she gasped and froze, her eyes wide.

As they'd all turned right to leave the stage, the light from Lauren's phone had illuminated a hideous sight.

Ben had been wrong.

This crawler was bigger than any they'd seen. Caught in

the light just as it had been sneaking up on them from the side, it reared on two of its metre-long legs; extending three more outward into the air around itself in a wide gesture of defiance it held itself there, poised, pale and quivering.

On its underside, instead of stingers there was a bizarre kind of three-sided beak: this opened like a flower, revealing a red mouth lined with white, incurving hooks and glittering with running slime. As Jasmine stood staring at the creature, transfixed with shock, Ben grabbed her, pulling her back. It was lucky he did, because the thing's beak or whatever it was suddenly jabbed a full metre straight out of its body and snatched at the space where she'd been standing with a *snap*.

'Go! Go! Get out! Everyone! *Now!*' gibbered Ben, finally regaining the power of speech. Samantha and Lauren were already on their way so, yanking on Jasmine's arm to send her off ahead of him, he ran.

Wham. WHAM! Two more of the giant crawlers dropped onto the stage from the lighting rigs above. Ben heard seats being flipped all over the theatre: as he charged up the stairs to the exit he glanced back and saw a converging ripple in the auditorium as even more of them gave chase.

'Run! *Run! RUN!*' he yelled, whether to the girls or himself he wasn't sure. Nobody needed further prompting. The theatre doors banged back on their hinges and swung shut, but no one even thought of trying to seal or block them this time, they just kept running – back up the stairs, back to the foyer's upper level.

Ben ran into the choking gas at full pelt, careless of the battle still raging by the main entrance. The girls were ahead, Jasmine nearest: when she suddenly stopped Ben ran straight into her, his flailing arms connecting with two other bodies as he did so.

'Sorry!' he spluttered. 'Sorry!'

'Come on!' yelled Samantha, frantically punching at the wall. 'Come on, come on, *come on*!'

Magically, to Ben's astonishment, sliding doors parted in the fog. A downward-pointing arrow winked on. Lights beckoned from inside the elevator cubicle. Ben and the three girls piled in.

'*Doors closing*,' the lift announced in its female voice. '*Lift going down*.'

11:38 PM.

I squirmed in my pit. Twenty-two minutes remained until Steadman's bombs were due to detonate. I confess, I was anxious.

I needed only to keep intruders out of the Barbican for just a little longer. But it was fully armed, fully trained soldiers who were being sent against me now.

I had been careful to choose and retain the strongest of my subjects, keeping them from the attentions of my drones. Even so, my defensive forces were down to half what they had been. The subjects who remained were loyal of course, and touchingly careless of their own safety in their desire to serve me. There were, however, few trained fighters among them, and most were unarmed.

It was fortunate, therefore, that my *newest* subjects were soldiers themselves.

In the lull after beating back the latest incursion, two of these suited men broke away from the pack. Bringing their guns with them they quickly climbed the stairs and – with no direct prompting from me – posted themselves on the balcony. While my main force returned to their positions once more to prepare for the next wave of attack, I watched through the two soldiers' eyes as they took aim, covering the foyer entrance.

Their positioning was perfect. The gas was clearing: they had a commanding view. Now any armed intruder who proved too troublesome could – to use a vivid term I'd just gleaned from the two soldiers' minds – be 'slotted' from cover.

I had snipers. I adore it when my subjects use their own initiative.

In the pit I settled back as comfortably as I could. The

cocoons were protected and soon they would hatch. I had only to wait for my young human *protégée* to come for me.

Twenty-one minutes, now.

11:39 PM.

'You saved us, babes!' said Lauren to Samantha, eyes shining.

'How?' asked Jasmine. 'How did you know where to go in the fog?'

'You're not the only one with ideas around here,' Samantha told her.

'Let's hope yours are better than mine,' said Ben with feeling. 'The theatre was a *bad* suggestion. Sorry, everybody.'

'What *were* those things?' Samantha asked.

'Which things?' Ben asked back. 'The big crawlers or the cocoon-things?' Realizing how stupid he sounded, he scowled and banged his fist against the cubicle's metal wall. 'I just wish we could find out what's going on!'

'Those cocoons,' said Samantha quietly. 'You're sure they've got people inside?'

'You saw the shoes,' said Jasmine. 'Men. Women. Schoolkids.' She paused. 'Maybe that's why, apart from Hugo and Lisa, we haven't seen any kids with crawlers on them, just adults. Maybe all the other kids are in there.' She shivered.

'But what're they doing, all wrapped up like that?' asked Samantha. 'What's going to happen to them?'

'Maybe they're dead,' said Ben. 'Or . . . maybe something worse.'

'Wh-what are you talking about?' asked Lauren, quailing.

'Never mind,' said Jasmine firmly.

There was a pause.

'Well,' she added as brightly as she could, 'at least now we're in this lift we can try some different floors. Where are we going first?'

'I thought we'd start at the bottom,' said Samantha.

'Sounds appropriate,' said Ben. 'We're pretty much at rock bottom ourselves, right? I mean, it's not like things could get much worse.'

'Stop it, Ben!' said Jasmine, annoyed. 'Of course things could be worse. We're still free, aren't we? We haven't been caught yet. We're doing all right!'

Ben had known what he was saying was unhelpful even as he'd said it. Chastened by Jasmine's refusal to give in to the bleakness of their situation, he looked at his feet.

'Sorry,' he said, again.

Maybe Josh would have handled all this better, he

thought. Josh almost never seemed down or discouraged; that was one of the things Ben found most annoying about him. How were Josh and Robert doing anyway? he wondered. Was Lisa was still unconscious? But then Ben noticed that the lift was slowing to a halt.

'OK,' said Jasmine. 'Get ready on the buttons. If anything bad happens we need to be able to shut the doors and get out of here as quickly as possible.'

'Yes, *thank you*, Jasmine,' said Samantha. 'I had worked that out for myself, you know.'

The doors slid open.

There was no forest of arms reaching in to grab them. There was no choking smoke, no gunfire and no crawlers, big or small – or none they could see. Instead, the room that the doors had opened to reveal was . . . empty.

Ben, Jasmine, Samantha and Lauren just stood there looking out. The room was silent, a silence Ben didn't want to break, and for once even Samantha and Lauren seemed to share the feeling.

To the immediate right of the lift doors was a wall that was covered in mirrors. The Barbican's usual bare concrete loomed from the ceiling, and the same 'blue worms trodden into grey mud' carpet stretched off for some ten metres to the left before turning right round a corner: the room was a sort of L-shape. It was brightly lit and clean. Of what was going on in the rest of the building it bore no signs whatsoever. It was just an empty room.

The lift's female voice was the first to speak: '*Doors closing,*' it said. The panels began to slide shut – but they stopped on Samantha's foot, and retreated.

'Looks clear out there,' she said. 'Who wants to come and check it out?'

'I'll come!' said Lauren, with hysterical enthusiasm.

'At least one of us should stay by the lift,' said Jasmine. 'It looks all right here, but we might need to make a quick getaway.'

'Suit yourself,' said Samantha. She and Lauren set off.

'Be careful!' said Jasmine, but they were already around the corner and out of sight. She sucked her teeth. 'Honestly. Those two . . .'

'*Oh my God!*'

Lauren's sudden shout froze Ben's blood.

'What?' Jasmine yelled back. 'Lauren, what is it? What have you found?'

'They have a *girls' toilet* down here!' was Lauren's delighted reply. 'Oh, thank God. I was going to wet myself!'

Ben and Jasmine stared at each other. Ben smirked; Jasmine's lower lip trembled. Then they both cracked up.

It could have been shock – the unrelenting horror of the evening finally overcoming them both. It could have been the contrast between the basic humanity of Lauren's reaction and the dreadful things they'd witnessed. Or it could just have been the fact that they needed a laugh: Ben didn't know and didn't care. He and Jasmine giggled until they were breathless.

'I'll stay,' said Ben chivalrously, once he'd got himself together.

'Thanks,' said Jasmine, smiling back at him.

When Ben was alone in the lift he sat down on the floor with his back to the edge of the sliding door. Every ten seconds for the next few minutes the hydraulics would nudge him gently.

'*Please do not obstruct the doors*,' the lift's voice commanded. '*Please do not obstruct the doors.*'

Ben kept watching the corner even after Jasmine had gone around it. His sides and lungs ached – from laughter or gas or both – but his heart felt like it was glowing.

Jasmine was beautiful, she was clever, she was brave and cool in a crisis, and now Ben knew that she could laugh about things: Jasmine was *awesome*. He had felt it when he'd first locked eyes with her. OK, having an ice cream land on his head wasn't the best introduction, and he'd really thought he'd screwed things up that time she'd called him smug. But there was a connection between them – wasn't there?

Ben certainly hoped there was but, nerve-rackingly, he couldn't be sure. Ben was usually fairly confident around girls

– a natural by-product of growing up with two bossy older sisters. But whenever he was close to Jasmine and they *weren't* running for their lives, that confidence seemed to desert him.

At any rate, Samantha's warnings earlier about Jasmine being a traitor now seemed like a sick joke or bad dream. There was no doubt in Ben's mind: if they ever got out of this, he was definitely going to try to get to know Jasmine better.

If they got out of this, his brain whispered back to him.

Ben's smile faded.

I like him, thought Jasmine. Sure, Ben had faults. He could be cocky. He could be gloomy. He was a little aloof, detached from things – which probably made him seem a bit cold and self-possessed sometimes. *But that*, Jasmine told herself, *sounds quite a lot like someone* else *we know – right?* In fact she and Ben seemed to have quite a lot in common: not just because they were outsiders in their schools, but in the way they acted, the way they thought. He was brave, he was quick on the uptake, *and* he was cute. She wondered how he felt about her . . .

Jasmine was round the corner now. The sight of stairs leading up to the right brought her up short: she suddenly realized that this was the bottom flight of the main stairs, the ones they'd been on earlier before the adults had chased them out at the balcony level. She bit her lip. She hoped that those people (*the ones who weren't cocooned*, she reminded herself, shuddering) were all up there in the foyer, still fighting. If any of them happened to come thundering down those steps, she didn't fancy her and Lauren's and Samantha's chances of getting back to Ben and the lift.

Not far from the bottom of the stairs were three doors. To Jasmine's left was one marked CINEMA. To her right was the entrance to the Ladies, marked by another illuminated sign over the door. Ahead, the third door was marked (of all things) THE PIT.

Wow, ominous much? Jasmine thought. Suppressing a small shudder, she pressed on the heavy swing door to the lavatories, and went through . . .

Into darkness. After the bright light outside Jasmine was so surprised that she forgot to hold the door open: when it swung shut behind her she was stranded. She'd just begun to grope blindly for the door handle when the overhead strip lights flickered on, then off again.

Jasmine froze. In the flash of light, she'd seen that the room was long and narrow, with cubicles to the left and a row of basins on the right. In front of the basins, arms crossed, stood Lauren and Samantha – waiting for her.

'You startled me,' said Jasmine, with an easiness in her voice that she didn't remotely feel. The lights flicked on, then off again. The other girls hadn't moved. 'What's up with the lights?'

'You took your time,' said Samantha.

'Yeah!' sneered Lauren, taking what she obviously saw as her cue. 'Wanted to be alone with your lover boy?'

Jasmine did not reply. The way the lights kept flickering on and off was very disorienting. Sometimes they would stay on for one or two seconds at a time, sometimes less. With the darkness and the retina-flashes they left behind it was as if the whole room was strobing. Otherwise though, oddly, the scene was familiar.

It felt a lot like Jasmine's school. At break times the toilets were where Samantha held court, with Lauren as her loyal retainer. If it weren't for the flickering lights – and everything else, of course – this could almost be a situation Jasmine encountered every school day. *Weird*, she thought.

She deliberately walked past Lauren, ignoring her, and went into the nearest cubicle – without passing Samantha. There was something about the set of Samantha's mouth and the way she was standing there that made Jasmine not want to get too close to her. Jasmine shut and locked the cubicle door.

'What's the deal with you and Ben, anyhow?' Samantha asked, from outside.

'What are you talking about?' Jasmine asked back, still trying to keep her voice light.

'Don't try to deny it!' crowed Lauren. 'You've been eyeing him up all night – don't think we haven't noticed!'

'What's it to you two, anyway?' asked Jasmine mildly, frowning at the door.

'We know you, Jasmine,' said Samantha. 'The way you've been acting, playing the leader – it's not like you. Is it all for his benefit? Or is it something else?'

'Samantha,' asked Jasmine, opening the cubicle door, 'are you *still* carrying on with that stuff about how I'm a traitor in the group? I mean, do you really believe that? Or are you just annoyed because you're not the one in charge?'

The lights had flicked off again – for a long while this time. Apart from the blue-green flashes on her retinas, Jasmine had asked her questions in the dark.

'You're right,' she heard in reply. 'Samantha's not in charge. But then, neither are you.' There was a rustling, skittering noise in the surrounding blackness. *'I am.'*

'Babes?' asked Samantha uncertainly. 'What are you on about? Why's your voice gone funny? What— *Ow! What are you doing?'*

The lights flickered on again, and Jasmine saw that Lauren had now grabbed Samantha by her arms, high up, near her shoulders. The two girls stood like that, face to face.

'Lauren hates you, you know,' said Lauren's mouth – but the voice that came out of it was not Lauren's. It was unfamiliar – deeper, older. 'She only pretended to look up to you because she needed your protection.'

'Wh-what?' said Samantha.

'Did she never tell you about the note?' Lauren's mouth smiled. 'I thought not. At Lauren's previous school all the children in her class signed a little message: *We all hate you*, it said. A small thing, but Lauren never got over it. Believing she wasn't strong enough by herself, when she started at your school she attached herself to you, Samantha. But then, tonight, just after eight o'clock, *I* gave Lauren something better.'

'Jasmine!' yelled Samantha, starting to struggle, but the grip that held her was inescapable. One finger at a time, a crawler came into view over her shoulder. '*Help me!*'

The creature positioned itself on Samantha's neck, then struck. Lauren's hands released their grip. As Samantha dropped to the floor like a rag doll the lights flicked off again.

Until this moment Jasmine had stood rooted to the spot, barely believing what she was hearing and seeing. Now, at last, she launched herself out of the cubicle and lunged for the door, flailing blindly for its handle in the darkness. Of course she was too late.

'No, Jasmine,' she heard. 'I've something special planned for you.'

She felt a hand on the back of her neck.

Then, when Jasmine understood what it really was, she screamed.

***

Ben was already up off the floor and running.

'Ben!' he heard. 'Help! Quick! *Ben!*'

The lift doors closed behind him but he didn't even notice. His eyes were only on the girl who had just staggered into view.

'Lauren?' he asked. 'What is it? What's the problem? What's going on in there?'

'It's *Jasmine*,' Lauren wailed. 'She . . . changed. Then crawlers came out of the ceiling, and they got Samantha, and . . .' she choked and fell against him heavily. 'Oh, *Ben!*'

'Take it easy,' said Ben, putting his arms around her awkwardly. 'Um, what are you saying? Tell me again slowly.'

'It was true, Ben!' said Lauren, staring into his eyes. 'Samantha was right: there *was* a traitor. She was bitten right at the beginning. She's had a crawler on her the whole time: Ben, it was *Jasmine*!'

'*What?*' asked Ben, horrified, looking past Lauren at the door to the Ladies. 'Really?'

'No,' said Lauren, in a deeper voice. She produced the fresh crawler she'd been holding at her side and put it on the back of Ben's neck. 'Not really.'

Ben felt its bite, like two hot needles being shoved under the base of his skull. He went rigid, helpless.

'I had thought that tricking you into mistrusting Jasmine

would be harder, Ben,' said Lauren's mouth, making a *moue* of disappointment. 'Perhaps the two of you aren't becoming as fond as you seem.'

'I . . .' Ben croaked, staring up at the camera on the ceiling.

Then everything went black.

11:42 PM.

Jasmine returned to consciousness in darkness, but the first thing she noticed was that she was standing up.

OK, she thought, *that's kind of odd.*

Her eyes felt dry, so she blinked – or rather her brain sent the message to her eyelids, but nothing happened. The same thing occurred when she tried to lift her hands to rub her eyes: the hands remained at her sides without even so much as moving a finger. She tried to open her mouth – even to twitch her tongue: nothing. Jasmine was just standing there, like a mannequin waiting to be positioned.

Her body was no longer her own. She began to panic.

The lights flickered on overhead, revealing Lauren's face, just centimetres from hers.

'Yes,' said Lauren – or rather what was controlling her. 'This is exactly why I never allow my subjects as much awareness as this. It's too distressing for them. But you, Jasmine, you're not like the others, are you?'

They were in the toilets, but Jasmine didn't care about her surroundings. Inside, she was screaming. She was utterly helpless. She still had sensations – hunger, fatigue, a persistent itch at the sides and back of her neck – but her mind was only *receiving* these signals. She was incapable of sending anything back. Her body was a prison. Jasmine was locked inside her head, every bit as securely as if she'd been locked in a cage.

'Are you as strong and clever as I'm hoping, Jasmine?' said Lauren's mouth. It smiled. 'This is where we find out. Let me explain . . .'

Lauren turned, untucking and lifting the back of her grimy white school uniform shirt to expose the clinging creature that lay nestled at the base of her spine.

With a mental spasm of revulsion, Jasmine realized why her neck itched so much.

'That's right. My hand is upon you. So now you, like this one' – Lauren's hand gestured at herself – 'are almost completely under my control. Where it becomes interesting, of course, is the "almost".'

Lauren's face loomed in Jasmine's vision. Lauren's eyes, and what looked out of them, stared into Jasmine's.

'You are resisting,' the voice stated. 'I would expect no less from you. If you were like the others – if there was a part of you that *wanted* to give up – then I would not be so interested in you. You see, I've been watching you over the course of the evening. You have intrigued me, Jasmine.'

The voice was deeper than Lauren's, slightly husky, with an easy, velvet musicality to it. But Jasmine was barely listening. Her mind battered against its limits like a prisoner hurling herself against the bars, screaming, crying, until she was dizzy with pain. Of course, it all happened in silence. Any outward sign of her struggle was impossible.

Lauren's lips formed into a small pout. 'I do not ask for your surrender,' she said. 'All I ask, for now, is a truce.' She leaned forward until her lips were next to Jasmine's ear. 'Don't you want to know what's really happening here, and who is behind it all? Hmm?'

Wrenching her mind back into focus, Jasmine tried to calm down. When Lauren's face came back into sight, she was smiling again.

'That's better,' she said. 'Oh, that's *much* better.' Then: 'Let's go.'

The overhead lights flicked off again, but Jasmine found that she was already turning. Her hand reached out, found the door handle easily in the pulsing dark, and pulled.

Jasmine walked out – but Jasmine herself had nothing to do with any of it. She was aware of every movement: she was aware of the air around her and the way it moved across her skin. But the movements themselves did not come from her. She was being controlled.

'There,' said the voice from behind her, 'you're becoming accustomed to it already. But . . . Oh. Yes, of course.'

Jasmine had caught sight of Ben.

A part of her had been hoping desperately that he might have escaped somehow – that he might still be free, hiding in the building somewhere, figuring out a way to rescue everyone. Instead he was standing at the bottom of the stairs, with a crawler clamped to his neck. He stood there with his back to her – ignoring her. His hands, by his sides, were clenched into fists. Jasmine felt a soft pang of despair.

'I sent Samantha to join the battle upstairs,' said Lauren's mouth. 'I left Ben here on guard. Forget him. He can't help you; nobody can. Now let me show you why.'

Then Jasmine was walking again. As she passed Ben she wanted to keep looking at him, but her head wouldn't turn. She and Lauren were going towards the door she'd noticed earlier – the one that said THE PIT.

Lauren held it open for her, then followed her through.

11:45 PM.

'We have to do something,' said Robert.

He and Josh were standing in the monitor room. Between

them they'd at last got the hang of the console. They'd had trouble keeping Ben and the girls in sight in the fog of the foyer, but had found them again in time to witness what had happened. They had seen Lauren put the crawler on Ben. They had seen where Lauren and Jasmine had gone.

'Come on,' said Robert, when Josh didn't reply. 'I'm sick of waiting. Let's you and me go and *do* something, for a change.'

Josh turned and raised an eyebrow. 'Robert,' he asked, 'are you having some sort of episode? When we first came up here, you were crying like a baby. Now, what? You're an action hero?'

'No,' said Robert. 'All I'm saying is—'

'Yes, I heard what you're saying.' Josh's lip curled in disdain. He pointed at the screens. 'Robert, the *army's* down there – people with guns. But here you are, suddenly getting the urge to ride in and save the day. *You*, Robert. Wow, if this wasn't so pathetic I'd be laughing.'

'Coward,' said Robert.

Josh frowned. 'Excuse me?'

Robert's face was red with emotion. 'You heard. Lauren may have tricked Ben and Samantha and Jasmine, but at least they *tried*. All you do is sit there waiting to be rescued and telling people what to do.' He shook his head. 'And I used to think you were so great. Well, see you.'

He turned and set off.

'Robert . . .' said Josh, following him into the security room. 'Robert, your arm's broken. What exactly do you think you're going to do? You won't even get out of that door! Robert, come back!'

With his good right hand Robert opened it, revealing the empty passage beyond.

'The sentries are gone,' he told Josh, 'you *knob*.' He nodded at the unconscious body of Lisa. 'Stay here with her.'

With that, he left.

Josh stood there for a moment. He looked down at Lisa. Then:

'Robert?' he called. 'Robert! Wait for me!'

11:46 PM.

Jasmine passed through another set of doors and entered a dimly lit room. Rising to her right were twelve rows of empty seats. A metal frame holding a lighting rig hung from the ceiling.

The Pit was a theatre. It wasn't anything like as big and impressive as the one upstairs, nor was it supposed to be: this was a studio theatre, used for smaller-scale, more intimate productions.

'There's a story about this place and how it got its name,'

said Lauren's mouth. 'They say the Barbican was built on one of London's *plague pits* – a mass grave for victims of the Black Death.'

Helplessly Jasmine followed Lauren across the performance space, through a gap in a blackout curtain and into the Pit Theatre's backstage area. Jasmine passed some painted wooden boards and a pile of steel scaffolding poles – theatrical scenery of some kind, apparently abandoned in mid-construction. In the far wall, flanked by two open, plain, black doors with signs on them saying WARNING: AUTHORIZED PERSONNEL ONLY, she saw a tunnel.

'Elements of that story are true,' said the voice. 'The Barbican Centre is built over a pit. The pit was dug at the time of the Great Plague – the epidemic that ended in sixteen sixty-six. As to what the pit really contains, however . . . well, you're about to find out.' Lauren's body stood to one side of the tunnel entrance, and gestured. 'After you.'

The tunnel was a twenty-metre-long downward-sloping tube of bare, grey Barbican concrete. The air coming up from it was cold and damp and smelled of sewage. The tunnel did not seem to Jasmine like a good place to be. But her reluctance made no difference: her legs began to plod down it just the same.

'Sixteen sixty-six,' the voice behind her repeated. 'The Great Fire of London. If even Lauren here knows the date all British schoolchildren must do, one imagines. But what you don't know is that the fire was started *deliberately*.'

The tunnel's slope was too steep to walk down comfortably: with each step Jasmine's toes pressed hard against the ends of her school shoes, and her ankles and calves quickly began to ache. While she waited to arrive wherever her stolen body was taking her, Jasmine thought about Lauren. Had there been some clue, some giveaway word that Jasmine could have picked up on earlier? Perhaps. *But*, Jasmine wondered bleakly, *how could she have known?* To Jasmine, Lauren had always just been Samantha's pet – sucking up to Samantha in return for the protection of being with her. Jasmine had never felt any wish to get to know Lauren well enough to have noticed anything different about her tonight. Neither, it seemed, had Samantha.

'The city's owners, the Corporation of London, started the blaze to flush me out,' the voice went on. 'Imagine it: a whole city on fire for three days! I never could have guessed they would go to such lengths. But it worked. Here, under what is now called the Barbican Estate, is the northernmost point the fire reached. They had destroyed my hiding places, forced me out into the open. This was where they caught me.'

Jasmine had reached the end of the tunnel. To her right lay a massive round steel door of the kind used in bank vaults: presumably there to seal off the tunnel when closed, the door now lay open, flush with the wall. To Jasmine's left was a domed chamber.

It looked like a shallow, upside-down bowl. It wasn't especially high – perhaps five metres at the dome's highest point – but it was very wide, something like thirty metres in diameter. The walls, the ceiling and some of the floor were constructed entirely of pinkish red brick. The bricks looked old: they were worn, bulged outward by subsidence in some places, blackened with mould in others. But the chamber also featured some incongruous-looking modern touches. On the other side of the chamber Jasmine saw another round steel door, also standing open. A ring of chrome-sided light globes were bolted onto the wall, together with what looked like PA speakers and several types of camera, all angled inward.

In the centre of the room, taking up a good two-thirds of the floor space, was a wide circle of reinforced glass. Lauren walked out into the chamber until she was standing at the glass circle's edge.

'*This* is what gave the theatre its name,' said Lauren's mouth. 'This is the pit where the Corporation held me prisoner for almost three hundred and fifty years. *This* is where they insulted my person, with fire and steel and . . . devices. But no more. Tonight I leave this place behind for good.' Lauren pointed past Jasmine. 'Press that button, please.'

Jasmine turned, and found herself looking at a wall-mounted plastic box with a large red button in its centre. Her thumb pushed the button almost before she herself had seen it.

'Now wait there,' said the voice behind her, over the rising whine of machinery.

Jasmine did as she was told. She didn't have any choice. All she could do was stand there, looking at the wall, listening.

For ten slow seconds the sound of the machine continued; to Jasmine, it felt longer. Then, with an echoing hiss, it fell silent.

Jasmine waited.

There was a sudden great *rasp*, as if something large, heavy and wet was being dragged across the floor. This was followed by a snort, then a low crooning sound that was somewhere between a wheeze and a moan.

With no control over where her eyes went, Jasmine focused on her other senses. As well as the sewage smell she'd noticed earlier there was now a sudden extra noxious tang in the air – raw chicken, bad armpits, or some unholy mixture of the two.

Raaaaasp – that sound again, then the same deep, wheezing, booming moan of effort. Both were louder this time, and Jasmine sensed a definite increase in the smell's potency.

Jasmine knew what was happening: something was coming

up behind her – something big. She did not enjoy waiting for whatever it was to come into view. If she'd had any choice in the matter, she would be running. But she couldn't even shiver. She had to stand there as the sounds got closer, powerless to do anything but wait and see whether the truth behind the sounds was as horrifying as what they did to her imagination.

RAAAAASP. The smell was even stronger now – almost unbearable. The moan, when it came, was close enough for Jasmine to feel a warm exhalation on her back.

'There,' said the voice, from what felt like just beside her ear. '*Now* you may look on me.'

When Jasmine turned, the first thing she saw was the all-too-familiar figure of Lauren. But there was something strange about her. Was Lauren . . . taller? She was looking down at Jasmine and grinning – a wild, cruel grin that showed all her teeth. Jasmine's eyes travelled downward, and that was when she noticed that Lauren was *up off the ground.* Her feet were dangling in the air, her legs swinging gently.

Then Jasmine saw why.

Oh. My. God.

Jasmine's first impression was of a sort of hulking boulder shape, perhaps three metres across. But instead of rock, this thing was made of flesh. It was milky white in colour. Rings of grey muscle striped its rubbery sides. On the bit nearest to Jasmine was a primitive tube of a mouth from which projected a thick, dirty-grey, glistening tongue. The tongue had attached itself to Lauren's back somehow: it was this that was holding Lauren in the air.

Lauren's eyes seemed to glow as they stared down at Jasmine. Her arms lifted from her sides. Her terrible grin widened.

'Behold,' said her mouth, 'your Queen.'

11:48 PM.

Protect the Queen, said Ben's brain. Then again: *Protect the Queen.*

He was standing guard at the bottom of the stairs. This was his place – his line in the sand. He would allow no one to pass him. If anyone tried, he would stop them. Ben would fight – fight until he was dead if he had to – and he wouldn't die easily. He would fight until his last breath, until the last drop of blood left his body. He was protecting the Queen. And the Queen, to Ben, was everything.

The Queen's hand was upon him, laid gently on the back of his neck. She was there on the inside of Ben's head too, behind every thought. She was with him, cold and calm and ageless – watching through his eyes, keeping his thoughts straight, smoothing away anything that was complicated. For that, he loved her.

Ben loved how easy everything felt, now that the Queen

was with him. It was simple: where there had been fear, now there was certainty. Where there had been doubt, now there was clarity – freedom. Ben felt so light, so full of energy, that he thought he might actually lift off into the air. He stood there at his post at the bottom of the stairs, absolutely and utterly still, and the deliberateness of that lack of movement was like a charge of electricity building up in his chest. His blood seemed to crackle and fizz in his veins. Protect the Queen. Fight for the Queen. There was nothing else he wanted.

And now, he thought, instantly spotting the shadow that moved on the wall at the top of the stairs, *here comes my chance* . . .

The shadow loomed larger, became a full-sized silhouette, then a face was poking around the corner on the landing. The face was earnest and worried, round and a bit pudgy. It was also familiar.

'Ben?' said the face. 'Ben? Can you hear me? It's me . . . Robert.'

Ben didn't attack. Ben said nothing – just stayed still, watching.

Robert took a cautious step down the stairs towards him.

'Ben,' he said, pointing at him with his good arm, 'I know you've been bitten. You've got one of those things on you. I can see its . . . what do you call them – legs? They're right there on the sides of your neck.'

He was still walking down the stairs. He was only about six steps away from Ben now.

'I don't know if you can hear me,' said Robert. 'I don't know how this works, or if you can even understand what I'm saying. But in case there's any of you left in there, Ben, I have to take this chance . . .'

Ben's ears noticed a soft mechanical sound to his right somewhere, but he paid it no mind and certainly didn't turn. At that moment his eyes were rooted on Robert's feet.

On seeing Robert, Ben's wonderful certainty had wavered. Now he felt anxious. He should have attacked Robert on sight but he had hesitated: *why*? For a time Ben hadn't been able to think of an answer, which only made him *more* anxious. Now, however, he had hit on a way to be certain again.

Protect the Queen. So far, Robert had posed no threat: that was a reason not to attack. But he was on the last step now. If the toe of his shoe touched the floor at the bottom of the stairs, there would be no choice. If Robert set foot in Ben's kill zone, Ben would go for his throat.

'I just want to say *sorry*,' Robert said, still standing on the bottom step. 'We don't want to hurt you.'

The knowledge that there was something wrong with this statement was just penetrating Ben's mind when the noise to his right became suddenly identifiable as running footsteps.

'This isn't personal,' said Robert.

Then something crashed into Ben and he was knocked to the floor.

For a second he was so surprised that he didn't even react. There were hands on him. Someone was wrestling him and struggling with him, turning him on his back, trapping him under their weight. It wasn't Robert: Robert was still standing on the bottom step, looking anxious. Another face reared up in his vision. Josh.

While Robert had come down the stairs, Josh had used the lift. While Robert had been talking, keeping Ben distracted, Josh had snuck out of the lift then charged into Ben and tackled him to the floor. He was sitting astride Ben's chest, with his knees on Ben's arms – the classic playground fight position of dominance. And now . . .

'Now, Josh! Hit him! Knock him out!' yelled Robert.

Ben watched Josh's right fist swing down into his face.

The fist connected with Ben's left cheek, just on his lower jaw. His head, which was lifted forward at the time, flew back under the impact and bounced off the floor, but as it came up Josh was ready with another punch. A left this time, the punch connected with the right underside of Ben's chin and gave his neck a savage wrench as his head twisted helplessly under the blow. By chance the side of Ben's tongue happened to be between his teeth: upper and lower molars clashed together on it, crushing a centimetre-size chunk. His mouth filled with blood. When he turned to look up, Josh's right fist was already coming down again: Josh hit him a third time, then, breathing hard now, a fourth. Ben didn't resist, just took it. Josh was pulling back for a fifth when—

'Wait!' yelled Robert from the stairs. 'Maybe that's enough!'

Silence, broken only by the harsh gasp of Josh's breaths.

Ben opened his eyes, looked up at Josh, and smiled.

One of Ben's teeth felt loose, and his face was already starting to swell. It hurt him to smile at Josh, but the pain was worth it for the answering expression he saw on Josh's face. Josh had looked so determined while he'd been hitting Ben – the way he'd stared down at him, so fierce. Now, as Ben smiled up at him, he watched Josh crack again, his face revealing the ugly uncertainty and fear behind it once more.

Fight for the Queen. Die for the Queen. Ben opened his bloody mouth and screamed with joy.

Josh was kneeling on his arms, sitting on his stomach. But that wasn't going to hold back Ben. He gathered the electricity that had been building in his body and started to use it. With two short wrenching movements he freed his arms, planting his hands on the ground, elbows bent, to either side of himself. Then he began to sit up.

As soon as Josh felt the awful, remorseless strength inside Ben now he started hitting him again. But the punches were wild and desperate and Ben barely felt them. While Josh kept swatting at him, Ben sat all the way up. Ben planted his left hand on Josh's chest and continued to force him back – as if Josh's entire body weight was nothing. Josh had stopped hitting him now and was trying to wriggle away, trying to keep his balance as Ben pushed him, shrinking from Ben's touch, knowing what was going to happen. But Ben tightened his grip, bunching Josh's school shirt in his fingers. He got his knees underneath himself and climbed to his feet, lifting Josh with him.

Ben looked Josh in the eye, pulled back his right fist, and let fly.

The punch took Josh on the point of the chin. His head jerked back, the rest of his body went after it and he hit the floor.

Ben stood over him, fingers flexing. But Josh didn't move.

One punch was all it had taken to stop Josh: *one punch*. Ben howled his frustration. He wanted a *fight*. He wanted to rip Josh limb from limb, dance in his blood, force his fingers in through his ribcage and crush the life from his heart.

But then Ben remembered. He turned, looking for his other enemy.

Robert was standing at the bottom of the stairs, cradling his arm. When Josh first tackled Ben, he had taken the last step. He was now standing on the floor at the bottom of the stairs, his mouth hanging open.

Robert had trespassed and doomed himself. He was in Ben's kill zone – a legitimate target. He was a danger to the Queen and Ben had to act accordingly. Oblivious to the way it made the blood drip down the front of his school shirt, Ben grinned his widest grin.

Then he sprang.

11:49 PM.

'Am I not beautiful?' said the Queen, through Lauren's mouth.

Lauren's arms stretched wide. Behind her the creature that held her gave a delighted wriggle, quaking a full ten metres of milky blubber.

'Am I not *gorgeous*?' asked the Queen. 'Am I not truly the loveliest thing you ever saw in your life? Be honest now.'

Frozen in place, unable even to gag at the stench that surrounded her, Jasmine could not reply.

'*HAAAAAAAAAAAAAAH!*' a scream was forced from Lauren's lips. A burst of mechanical-sounding laughter followed – '*HAHAHAHAH!*' – and four great whoofing blasts of foul breath boomed from the Queen's own tube of a mouth.

'You find me repulsive,' the Queen stated. The prehensile tongue extended, lowering Lauren's face towards Jasmine's. 'But I *love* you, Jasmine. Of all my subjects so far, I love you the best. Walk with me.'

Grunting with effort, the Queen heaved the last of her bulk up out of the pit. Then (*RAAASP*, wheeze, moan) she set off towards the other steel door Jasmine had noticed earlier. Jasmine went with her. She had no choice.

To Jasmine, the Queen, big as she was, looked a lot like a maggot. She moved like one too: the grey hoops of muscle down her sides alternately swelled and contracted, manipulating different sections of her body to pull her along. The *RAAAASP* was the sound the Queen's rubbery flesh made as it dragged across the brickwork; the moaning and wheezing was a sign of how much effort that took. With each lurch forward, gobs of slime sprang out like sweat droplets all over the Queen's body.

'All this locomotion.' Lauren's mouth sneered in distaste. 'Most irksome. But necessary. This place is no longer safe. Fortunately an escape route has been provided.'

They were approaching the other steel door. Beyond it lay a passageway of dripping brickwork, and an intensifying stink of human waste that rivalled even the Queen's distinctive odour. As Jasmine's helpless steps took her over the lip of the door, she realized she'd been right: she *had* smelled sewage earlier.

The sewer was bigger than Jasmine had expected, perhaps fifteen metres across. Also, unusually for a sewer, it had lights: more of the same globes she'd seen in the pit chamber had been placed along the ceiling, leading away to her left. But a sewer was unmistakably what it was: a dark and reeking stream ran along a sunken concrete trough in its centre.

Still carrying Lauren, the Queen squeezed through the door after Jasmine. Turning her bulk with an effort, she started off up the tunnel, following the lights. Jasmine walked along at her side, unable to do anything else.

'You need to understand what I am giving you, Jasmine,' the Queen said. 'So now I will tell you something of who I am, and how I came to be here.

'Like you, in a way, I am a chosen child of fate. But I am the lone survivor of *trillions*. In the final cataclysm of her death my mother scattered us like seeds across the universe. Our chances were slim. Many us of were destroyed – crushed to nothing by the vagaries of gravity, or scorched to dust by angry stars. Many, many more of us simply drifted for ever, falling through blackness endlessly, to nowhere. Of even those few that made safe landing, most fell on barren ground – desolate places, devoid of life. But I, Jasmine, fell somewhere *far* more promising . . .

'For tens of millions of years I lay hidden, waiting for your kind to become worthy to serve me. By sixteen sixty-six (by your current calendar) your species was ready. Perhaps *too* ready: before I could establish my rule, the Corporation discovered my existence and took their steps to stop me. But they were greedy and secretive, and they coveted my power for themselves. Though the Great Fire razed huge swathes of London, the Corporation succeeded in flushing me out and capturing me without the general population ever realizing the Fire's true purpose. In the Corporation's furtiveness shall lie my strength. Now, when the mass of humanity knows me, it will be because they will already have become my subjects.

'Before her death sent me on my journey, my mother was Queen of Everything. I am her heir. With your help, Jasmine, I will claim my birthright. And this world shall be my capital.'

11:50 PM.

Robert backed away, holding his good hand palm out to ward Ben off. His foot caught on the bottom step: he tripped and fell flat on his back up the stairs.

Howling, Ben pounced. His knees were either side of Robert's chest. His hands closed eagerly around Robert's throat.

Robert's pudgy features, pocked with sweat, loomed up in Ben's vision. Disgust engorging his fury, Ben dug his thumbs into the loose flesh under Robert's jaw: he felt little rolls of neck-fat swell out between his fingers as he began to squeeze.

Robert's cheeks reddened quickly. His eyes bulged and turned bloodshot. His neck was hot under Ben's crushing hands, and Ben imagined the breath and the life that were trapped there. Robert's lips were moving, mouthing something. Ben stared into Robert's eyes, at the pleading in them.

He hesitated again.

Ben's orders were clear. The love of the Queen depended on him carrying them out. But while he had been more than happy to fight for her against Josh, fighting Robert was a different story. All his certainty was gone. In its place was churning nausea. Something inside himself was . . . resisting.

Ben didn't understand it. Until a moment before, everything had been simple: no decisions, no consequences. All he had to do was obey, and obedience was joy. *Kill him*, said his brain. *Kill him now, and make things simple again.*

But somehow Ben just wouldn't do what he was told. Following all orders unquestioningly, like a good subject, just . . . wasn't in Ben's nature.

He frowned, and in that moment Robert reached up with his good hand and yanked the crawler from Ben's neck.

Ben's eyes rolled back in his head. His hands went slack and he sank forward, insensible.

For several seconds there was silence. Robert just lay there breathing. Pain was like a grinding white light in his skull and something was wrong with his eyes. The bare concrete ceiling above him was only visible at the wrong end of a telescope full of darkness that juddered with the pulse of his blood.

Ben's head lolled with grotesque intimacy over Robert's left shoulder: Robert was trapped. Worse still, Ben was lying on Robert's broken arm, which Robert had been holding across his chest when he'd fallen. When he foolishly tried to use the arm to shift Ben, the pain flared and the darkness in his eyes threatened to swamp him. If it hadn't been for what he was holding in his good hand, he might have passed out.

Robert's hand was at his side, palm up, so the crawler was upside-down. It was twitching madly, thrashing its legs as it tried to right itself and find another victim – which, if he didn't keep a good grip on the vile thing, would certainly be Robert himself.

He took some more deep breaths. He counted to ten. Then he got going. Wriggling and twisting his hips, he managed to get himself out from under Ben, who rolled over, arms flopping. Then, still holding the crawler, Robert sat up on the steps.

Oof. The telescope effect in his eyes screwed inward and an ominous wave of sweaty cold ran through his body. But he still didn't pass out, so carefully, deliberately, he put his wriggling burden under one of his thick-soled shoes and pressed down, hard.

The creature gave a satisfying *scrunch*, but Robert had

stomped one of these things before: he wasn't going to be tricked a second time. Keeping pressure on his foot, he grasped one of the crawler's finger-like legs – and pulled. He had to tug quite hard, twisting it and bending it back and forth, but eventually, with a snap, it came free and Robert tossed it into a far corner. With a lot of effort, he proceeded to do the same to the other four. Then he lifted his shoe off the squashed, legless body, swung his foot back, and booted the creature's remains away as far as he could.

All this time, Ben lay on the stairs beside him. Josh still lay where he'd been felled by Ben's punch. Wiping his hand on his school trousers, Robert looked from one to the other.

It's just you now, he told himself. *You're the only one left. Whatever you do, don't pass out. Mustn't pass out . . .*

11:51 PM.

The Queen paused. Lauren's brow creased into a distracted frown.

'Casualties,' said her mouth. The voice sounded surprised. 'I am fast running out of hands. But the battle in the Barbican foyer has served its purpose: that situation is about to be rectified.' Lauren's eyes stared into Jasmine's again. 'I have something else to show you.'

Just ahead of where the Queen had stopped, a long white

object was lying on the tunnel's brick floor. It was another of the mysterious cocoon-things Jasmine had seen in the Main Theatre.

'Allow me to satisfy your scientific curiosity, Jasmine,' said the Queen, extending her tentacle-tongue. Lauren's hands reached out and started to dig and tear at one of the object's rounded ends.

Jasmine heard a gooey *snap*, then the Queen pulled Lauren back. Lauren's expression was pleased.

'We are just in time,' said her mouth. 'Take a look.'

Jasmine didn't want to, but her feet shuffled obediently forward. Inside the cocoon was a man. Lauren's hands had just revealed his face.

'This is Mr Steadman,' said the Queen. 'Until tonight, he was the Corporation's leader.' Lauren's eyes glanced down at him. 'How are you feeling, Mr Steadman?'

The man's skin was grey and waxy-looking. Jasmine had been certain he was dead. That was bad enough, but what she felt now was even worse: Mr Steadman stirred. His eyes sprang open. His mouth split into a blissful grin and in a guttural, bubbling voice he said:

'Wonderful, my Queen. I feel *wonderful*.'

'The Corporation kept me all these years because they wanted my power for themselves,' the Queen explained. 'Steadman's predecessors never quite managed to bring themselves to risk releasing me, but Steadman did. Even though he did so because he thought he could control me, I feel I should thank him.' Lauren looked down at the man. 'Thank you, Steadman,' the Queen told him.

He did not reply.

'Naturally,' the Queen added, making Lauren smile, 'such a service deserves its reward. So I have granted Steadman one of the highest honours I can bestow upon my subjects.' Lauren's eyes looked into Jasmine's again. 'Like those you saw in the theatre, he has become my *surrogate*. He has offered up his body to me, as both sustenance and incubation place. And now,' she announced, 'he's ready to hatch.'

Jasmine began to be aware of a faint sort of sizzling sound. Her mind crawling with horror, she hoped at first that the sound's origin was the ever-running stream of sewage.

'How are the little ones, Steadman?' asked the Queen, through Lauren's mouth.

'They're . . . tickling, my Queen,' said Mr Steadman. 'I can feel them, all the way through me. They're like champagne bubbles, rising. They're . . . they're . . . oh, my Queen!'

The sound, which was like fat sizzling in a pan, was getting louder. The shape in the cocoon began to struggle and thrash. Jasmine wanted to turn away, to close her eyes – anything to avoid seeing what was about to happen – but she was helpless. She saw it all.

CRAWLERS

Mr Steadman went rigid, his face transfixed with a terrible delight. There was a series of clattering sounds like bursting bubble-wrap; then the cocoon was suddenly alive with movement, glittering as if its now-translucent sheath had turned into shimmering liquid. But it wasn't liquid. It was hundreds of thousands of tiny, wriggling bodies.

Baby crawlers were popping out all over Mr Steadman's torso and legs. They were burrowing out of their cocoon – and out of him. As Jasmine watched, one of the creatures climbed out of Steadman's right nostril and dropped to the brick floor. Including its five legs the newborn crawler was about the size of Jasmine's thumbnail. With a definite sense of purpose it made straight for the sewer channel, jumped in and was carried away by the stream. Before long its hundreds of thousands of siblings followed, a drifting trail of little floating bodies that stretched away from Mr Steadman's shrinking remains, as far as Jasmine's eyes could see.

Steadman's eyes had rolled back in his head: only the whites were now showing and his mouth hung slack. Jasmine stared down at his face. Even without the Queen's control, she would have found herself unable not to: apart from Steadman's head, some rags of clothes and some skin and bones, there was nothing left of him.

'There,' said the Queen, with quiet pride. 'Soon my hands will be in this city's water supply: when the theatre's hatchlings come and I make my escape, I will use it to spread through the whole population. I will choose more surrogates; there will be more hatchings. Within days there will be a "crawler", as you call them, for every living human on this planet – and here is where it started. Which, Jasmine,' the Queen added silkily, 'brings us back to you.

'I want a companion with whom to share my triumph. I offered the chance to Steadman, but he was . . . foolish. So, Jasmine,' the Queen told her, 'I have chosen you.

'Of all our subjects so far, you are undoubtedly the best candidate. You are young: your thinking is not yet stunted by the short-sighted concerns of the adults of your kind. Indeed, while your peers had already begun to succumb to trivialities, you, alone among them, kept your vision. You *care* about this world, Jasmine. That makes you the perfect person to help rule it.

'If I had succeeded in sixteen sixty-six, your world would be a very different place. It was never my intention to allow your species to cause so much harm to this planet. Think, Jasmine, of those billions of your kind who now consume and pollute with no thought but for themselves. You know they will not stop willingly – they love their comforts too much. Someone has to *make them*. That is what I offer you. As you've seen, most of my subjects do my bidding gladly. With your guidance and counsel to help direct them we could make this world blossom as never before. I, as Queen, would desire nothing more. The Earth must become a worthy seat from which to rule my empire.'

Lauren's mouth smiled. 'My hand is upon you, Jasmine. We see what is in your mind. You may respond.'

After all the Queen's long speeches, the silence that came then was sudden and strange.

How much of Jasmine's thoughts did the Queen have access to? Jasmine realized that she had no way of knowing.

The seconds ticked by. The Queen was waiting.

Stamping on everything else she was feeling as best she could, Jasmine concentrated, trying to form the only answer she could think of:

Choice, she thought.

Lauren's eyes blinked. 'What was that?'

Give me a choice.

'Why?' asked Lauren's mouth.

Because otherwise, thought Jasmine fiercely, *all I'll be to you is a* pet, *not a companion.*

'Ah,' said Lauren's mouth, with a shifty twitch. 'Yes, I suppose that is true.'

Jasmine concentrated again. *Take your hand off me*, she thought. *Otherwise no choice.* Then she waited.

From across the trench, Lauren's eyes gave Jasmine a searching look.

Jasmine squashed her feelings. She put a lid on all her other thoughts, blanking out everything except her request. What she was asking was fair, wasn't it? If the Queen really wanted a companion, not a slave, then Jasmine had to have a choice.

'You are implacable, Jasmine,' said the Queen, sounding amused. 'And I would not have you any other way. Very well.'

Jasmine felt a disgusting internal shifting sensation as the probosces were withdrawn from the inside of her skull. The movement was deliberate, careful, to prevent her from losing consciousness. The fingers at her neck loosened their grip, then the crawler that had held her dropped to the floor.

Jasmine sank to her knees. Released, her mind's responses to her situation poured out all over her body in a rush. Her heartbeat skyrocketed. She felt sick to her stomach. Cold waves of shock ran down her arms and the backs of her legs. But then, breathing hard, adrenaline pumping, she got up. Forcing her eyes away from Steadman's remains and the sewer-trench's wriggling contents, she stared up into Lauren's face.

'Well?' the Queen asked. 'As I believe I mentioned, this place is no longer safe. In just a few minutes now the building above us will be destroyed, together with everything and everyone in it. It is time to make your choice. Come rule with me, or you will die here. Which is it to be?'

Jasmine's crawler waited, crouching on the brickwork next to her right shoe. She stamped down on it, hard.

'I'd rather die,' she said.

Then she turned and ran.

11:52 PM.

Voices. A dull ache at the back of his neck; a terrible sticky taste in his mouth. Then: pain. Ben's face was throbbing. His skin felt tight from swelling: every pulse of his blood made him feel like his head was going to split. But his ears worked fine, so for a while he just lay there and listened.

'Get up,' said one of the voices.

'I *can't* . . .' sobbed the other.

'Can't or won't? Come on, Josh, he only hit you once.'

'What do you want from me? Just leave me alone!'

'If all you're going to do is roll around on the floor crying, maybe I should.' Then, more kindly, Robert's voice added: 'Please, Josh. I can't do this on my own.'

Coughing, gasping, Ben rolled onto his back and sat up. He was still on the stairs. A couple of metres away he saw Robert kneeling next to Josh, who was curled up in a foetal position on the Barbican carpet.

Now Robert and Josh were staring at him. And that was when Ben remembered what had happened. His hands tingled with the memory of being clamped around Robert's throat.

'He's getting up again!' Josh gibbered, sitting up and pointing at him. 'He's coming back! He's going to get us! He's . . . he's . . . *keep him away from me!*'

'Pull yourself together, Josh,' said Robert mildly. 'Ben doesn't mean us any harm, not any more. Do you?'

Ben felt sick. 'Robert,' he said, 'I . . . I don't know what to say. I nearly . . .'

'I know,' said Robert, touching the livid marks on his neck and giving Ben a rueful look. 'I was there, remember?'

'You nearly took my head off!' said Josh. 'If I've got *whiplash* because of you, I swear I'll—'

'Shut up, Josh,' said Robert. Then, to Ben: 'The point is, you resisted. I saw it in your eyes.'

Unable to meet Robert's, Ben looked down.

There was a short silence.

'All right,' said Robert, getting to his feet. 'Let's go.'

'Go where?' asked Josh.

'The Pit,' said Robert, pointing at the theatre doors. 'You saw where they went, on the monitors.'

'And why should we follow them?' asked Josh, not moving.

Following Robert's example Ben stood up, trying to ignore the way his muscles grated and shrieked as he did so.

'Because we've got to help Jasmine,' he said.

'We've got to find out what's going on here and stop it,' said Robert.

'We're going to find the Queen,' said Ben. Robert looked at him enquiringly, but Ben just nodded to himself. 'And when I find her,' he added, 'I'm going to kick her arse.'

'Splendid,' said Josh, from the floor. 'You two go ahead and do whatever you like.'

'Get up, Josh,' said Ben. 'You're coming too.'

'Or what? You're going to hit me again?'

'No,' said Ben, cracking another smile that hurt like hell but was worth it. 'But if you don't get up and by any chance we *do* get out of this, then we'll be sure to tell the whole school what a snivelling little weasel you really are.' Ben looked at Robert. 'Right?'

Robert smiled back.

11:55 PM.

I watched the girl as she ran back up the tunnel.

'Don't turn your back on me, Jasmine,' I called. 'Jasmine! I'm warning you!'

She ran on.

'*Where do you think you'll go?*' I asked as her footsteps echoed around me. 'Wherever you run, I will find you. And when I do, I'm going to *make you suffer*!'

At the vault door Jasmine paused, shoes skidding on the brickwork. She glanced back at me, then vanished from sight, back into the pit chamber.

I considered for a moment. Five minutes remained until Steadman's bombs were due to detonate.

My primary objective was complete. The Barbican had served its purpose. My subjects inside it had maintained a safe perimeter while my drones matured; the subjects had then continued to defend the building until those whom the drones had made surrogates reached the hatching stage. With the hatching accomplished, all I needed my remaining humans in this building to do was hold off intruders for long enough to cover my escape.

I was free. I had enough hands to rule the whole city. I was also safe, protected in these tunnels from the coming explosion by the weight of ancient London clay around and above me. I could leave – and in perfect secrecy. As Steadman had said, the bombs would eradicate all evidence of my existence. And yet . . .

Jasmine had *rejected* me.

I had never been rejected before. Admittedly, I had never allowed the possibility before. Why would I? Your kind are my subjects. I am your Queen. It is not your right to choose otherwise.

So why, I demanded of myself, *had I granted exactly that right to Jasmine?*

I hurt; I fumed. Then I decided.

Jasmine's insult could not be suffered to stand. The girl would pay for her insolence.

I set off after her.

Five minutes. It was going to be close.

Three minutes after passing through the door to the Pit Theatre, Ben, Robert and Josh were standing in an office. Ben was blinking, and now feeling unsure how much more weirdness he could take.

The office was built into the wall of a *secret underground chamber.* He and Robert and Josh had just discovered this chamber at the bottom of a tunnel that led down from the theatre's backstage area. And as well as the office's extra-ordinary location, there were other weird things about it, too. The room was dominated by a massive desk, the work surface of which was a large panel of sheer black glass. The glass worked as a flat screen. Like a flashier version of the monitor room, hundreds of camera feeds from all over the Barbican – and beyond – were displayed in a grid across the desktop. The walls of the office were covered in expensively framed photographs, and one man was present in all of them. Ben didn't recognize the man but he recognized some of the people with whom he was shown shaking hands: he counted

two prime ministers, several presidents and even – in one –
a pope.

'Who *is* this guy?' Ben asked, with feeling.

'That's Lionel Steadman,' said Josh. 'He's Alderman-in-
Chief of the Corporation of London. An extremely powerful
and influential man.'

'And how do *you* know who he is?' Ben asked.

'Didn't I tell you?' said Josh airily. 'My dad works for the
Corporation. Strange, isn't it? I wonder what Mr Steadman's
doing with an office down *here* of all places . . . What?' he
added, when he noticed the way Ben was still looking at
him.

Ben didn't answer.

'No,' said Josh firmly, shaking his head for extra emphasis.
'You don't think . . . ? No! The Corporation couldn't *possibly*
be responsible!' He started blinking rapidly. 'My . . . my *dad*
works for them!'

'Um, guys?' Robert interrupted, pointing at one corner
of Mr Steadman's desk. 'I think you should take a look at
this.'

The area of screen/desk Robert was indicating showed a
digital countdown, with (when Ben first saw it) four minutes
and thirty-eight seconds left to run.

TIME REMAINING UNTIL BARBICAN'S TOTAL DESTRUCTION,
said the title above it, helpfully.

Josh pointed and gulped. 'Th-that doesn't actually mean what it *says* it does. Does it?'

The boys stared at the countdown. Then they stared at each other.

The silence was broken by a sudden thump on the reinforced glass of the office's front wall. Ben jumped. Then he gaped.

'Jasmine?' he asked.

She was standing outside the office, panting slightly, her hands pressed against the glass, peering in. Ben ran round the desk, through the office door, and out into the pit chamber to meet her . . .

But Jasmine recoiled from him. For a long moment she stayed in a half crouch, ready to run again, her eyes wide, assessing him.

Ben froze, feeling sick. 'It's me,' he said sadly. 'Jasmine, I—'

Then she did something else he found totally unexpected. She lunged, grabbed him, wrapped her arms around him – and kissed him on the lips!

Ben was so astonished that he almost didn't know what to do. Feeling awkward, foolish, physically sore, but at the same time utterly delighted, he kissed Jasmine right back.

After only a second or two she pulled away. 'Ben!' she said, pressing her face to his chest. 'Oh God, Ben!'

Then . . .

Raaaaaaaasp.

Jasmine blinked, took a step back, but kept one hand on Ben's chest – as if she needed to be certain he was still really there.

'We need to get out of here,' she said.

'Um, absolutely,' said Ben, wrenching his mind back to thinking about the countdown.

'No, *seriously*,' said Jasmine. 'We need to start running. Right now.'

'Are you OK, Jasmine?' asked Robert, emerging from the office with Josh.

'No,' said Jasmine again. 'I am very, very far from OK. I've seen what's behind all this. I've seen what we're up against. And she's coming.'

RAAAAAAAASP.

'Jasmine?' said another voice. '*I see you!*'

Ben stared past Jasmine, past the empty pit, to the giant steel door on the other side of the chamber. Lauren was there. She was smiling – so widely that the pit chamber lights picked out the spittle strings glinting between her open jaws. And behind her, forcing her bulk back through the door into the chamber, was the Queen.

Ben knew her straight away. He had never seen the Queen but the aura she gave off was unmistakable: he recognized her presence at the back of his mind, remembered the dark and abject love he'd felt for her. The contrast between that and Jasmine's kiss a moment ago made him dizzy with revulsion.

'Stay where you are, all of you!' shouted the voice from Lauren's mouth.

Ben swore. Robert gulped. Josh's mouth fell open. Then they all took Jasmine's advice, and ran.

All four sprinted out of the other vault door and up the tunnel, back the way they'd come. To Ben it felt like he'd been running all night. He hurt all over. He was tired, he was hungry and he was scared. As he laboured up the steep concrete tube that led back up to the Pit Theatre he wondered how much running he had left in him. *When is it going to end?* he asked himself.

The answer came quicker than he expected. Jasmine reached the Pit Theatre's doors first, just ahead of the boys. She pulled the doors open: Ben saw past her, and realized they had already run as far as they could.

The room outside the theatre – the empty space with the doors to the toilets, the stairs, the lifts – had vanished. The concrete walls, the patterned carpet, even the ceiling: all had been smothered under a tumult of tiny, pale bodies.

Mr Steadman's cocoon had not been the only one to hatch, Jasmine saw: so, apparently, had all the ones in the Main Theatre. The newborn crawlers – millions of them by the look of it – had made their way down here, presumably intending to use the same escape route as the Queen.

Jasmine and the boys were cut off.

At least a dozen of the giant-size crawlers strode across the surrounding mass. Noticing Jasmine, four of them reared up, beaklike mouth-parts open and poised to snap. The nearest was barely half a metre away: the mass of creatures had reached the doors almost at the same time Jasmine had.

She flung the doors shut uselessly and backed away.

'Don't tell me,' said Josh with a humourless grin. 'We're trapped again, aren't we? Well that's brilliant. That's just brilliant. What are we going to do now? That . . . thing behind us, those things out there, and this time – oh, yeah – *the building's about to explode*!' He turned on Robert. 'What did you make me come down here for? Why didn't you just leave me alone? At least in the security room I wouldn't have known what was coming!'

'It's true,' said Ben to Jasmine. 'We found a timer in that office – some sort of countdown. It said that in just a few minutes the whole building's going to blow up.'

'The Queen said this place was no longer safe,' Jasmine murmured, almost to herself. She looked at her feet.

All night she had hidden her fear. All night she had stifled the urge to bury her head and start screaming. She had held herself together – always analysing, always working out what to do next, and whenever everyone had looked to her, which they had, almost constantly, she had always come up with answers. Even when she'd been alone, she had *still* come up with an answer to escape the Queen's clutches. But after finding Ben again – after kissing him and feeling so glad to be with him, to be alive – knowing now that they stood no chance . . . it was too much.

Jasmine had no more answers.

'That's it, then,' she said, nodding dully. 'We're done. Game over.'

Ben looked at Jasmine – her downcast eyes, the slump in her shoulders. For the four hours since everything had started Jasmine had been a pillar of strength – keeping her head in the midst of horror, chivvying the rest of the group – not least himself – into action instead of despair. Now, at last, it had happened: Jasmine had given up.

It twisted Ben's heart to see her like this. He wanted to say something: he wanted to come up with a brilliant plan that would get them all out of there, something that would make Jasmine smile at him again. But though he racked his brains, all he could think of was zombie films.

His love of horror films and games had helped keep him sane all night. Their logic, the way that characters in them reacted,

SAM ENTHOVEN

had given him clues about what to do. Now, all they told him was that the situation was hopeless.

The classic zombie movies all had unhappy endings. There was always a point where all the characters' efforts failed: the defences cracked, the horde broke through, all was lost. Ben had loved that about them. It seemed more truthful to him, more satisfying, than any superficial and lame attempt to impose a 'happy ever after'. So now, at what felt like the same point in his own story, Ben had nothing to say.

'Weapons,' said Robert.

'What?' said Jasmine.

'We need *weapons*,' Robert repeated.

Ben, and everyone else, stared at him.

'We need to find some way we can fight,' said Robert. 'Let's face it, it's either that or we just let them get us. And I want to do something. I don't care much what. Just as long as I know we *tried*.'

Josh snorted. 'That's it. Now I know you've gone mental. How do you think you're going to fight with your arm broken?'

'I don't know, Josh,' said Robert, gritting his teeth. 'But I'm open to suggestions.'

For another whole second Ben gaped at Robert. He would never underestimate him again. He closed his mouth.

'Robert's right,' he said, nodding at him coolly – or trying to. 'Let's look around. There's got to be some way to fight back.'

'Like what?' asked Jasmine.

BLAM! The theatre doors sprang back on their hinges.

'I don't know!' said Ben, his pretence at outward calm evaporating under a blowtorch of panic. 'Something! Anything!'

He turned and started hunting.

The Pit Theatre's backstage area didn't look promising. In fact it looked worse than the broom cupboard had been. Ben swore. It was so unfair!

If this had been a game, a first person shooter, there would have been weapons. The game's designers, knowing that a final 'boss' fight was coming up, would have left useful things strewn around the place – guns, ammo, extra health, stuff like that. But here, there were no grenades or rocket launchers. There weren't even any medical kits to magically restore his battered body to capacity. There was just him, and Jasmine, and Robert, and Josh . . .

And, he noticed, some scaffolding.

'There,' he said, pointing. 'What's that?'

Jasmine looked and saw a stack of painted wooden boards. She'd seen them before when she'd first come through here. 'What, the scenery?' she asked.

'No, these,' said Ben, moving towards the pile of steel poles that had been laid out in readiness for their job of *supporting* the scenery. He grabbed one of the short ones from the top of the pile and hefted it like a club.

The pole was about a metre long and slightly rusted – hollow, but heavy. Near the opposite end to where Ben was holding it a clamp was still attached, making it heavier still and very unwieldy, but if he could get in a couple of good swings with it maybe he could do some damage. He looked at Jasmine.

But she wasn't looking at him.

Jasmine gave the pile a kick, dislodging the smaller poles stacked on top: they tumbled all over the floor with an unmusical clanking sound – attracting the attention of Robert, who'd been fiddling vainly with a fire extinguisher he'd found attached to a nearby wall. He gave up, and came over to see what the noise was about.

At the bottom of the pile were half a dozen scaffolding poles that were much longer than the others. The longest was perhaps three metres.

'Ben,' said Jasmine, 'I think you've found it.'

Ben frowned, still grasping his makeshift club. 'I have?'

'Drop that,' said Jasmine, kneeling. She didn't smile, but a hard glint had entered her eyes. 'Josh? Robert? We need to work together now. This is going to take all of us . . .'

CRAWLERS

11:57 PM.

RAAAAASP. The sound of my body reverberated up the tunnel. The snort and wheeze of my breath had become a catarrhal gasping as I heaved myself after my prey. I am not accustomed to moving at speed. Nor to doing things for myself.

'You mean nothing to me, Jasmine,' I lied, through Lauren's mouth. 'Soon I will have this whole world from which to choose a companion. But I promise you, when my hand is upon you again, you will love me – *for the rest of your short but painful little life!*'

I stopped, breathing hard. At the top of the tunnel, just inside the entrance, stood a figure.

'Jasmine?' I asked, straining Lauren's eyes. 'Is that you?'

The figure didn't move.

'So . . . you came back,' I said. 'Changed your mind, have you?' I shaped Lauren's mouth into a sneer. 'What if it's *too late*, Jasmine? What if I'm not interested in you any more? What's a last-minute change of heart going to be worth *then*? Hmmm?'

The figure at the top of the tunnel didn't answer.

My own vocal organs were good for one thing: I laughed, making Lauren laugh with me – the human girl's cackling treble a counterpoint to the boom of my bass.

'I am jesting with you, Jasmine,' I said. 'Of course you can still be my companion.' I held out Lauren's arms. 'I forgive you. Come to me.'

The figure started running down the tunnel.

There was something odd about the way Jasmine was moving: her right hand was level with her hip, and her left arm was across her body. As I watched through Lauren's eyes Jasmine was joined by three more figures following along behind her: they too held their hands to one side, as if they were all . . . carrying something.

'Jasmine?' I asked uncertainly. 'What are you doing?'

'Aaaaaaaah!' Jasmine, Ben, Robert and Josh screamed at the top of their voices as they reached the target of their charge.

Then, like a harpoon, the tip of the three-metre-long scaffolding pole plunged past Lauren, straight into the Queen.

The pole was hollow. The circular edge of rusty steel at its tip wasn't particularly sharp, but with the weight of the pole itself plus that of four young people running down a slope with it, it was sharp enough. With a horrible, wet, puncturing sound it stabbed the Queen, driving almost a full two metres into her soft body.

'YEEEEEEEEEE!' A terrible, rending shriek pierced the air. The Queen bucked and thrashed. Instantly Ben and everyone else were knocked off balance, flung to the ground by the movement of the pole.

Ben stared upward in awe at what they had done.

Their spear had penetrated the Queen's tongue at its thickest point, where it jutted out of her mouth. Now the dirty-white meat of the tongue was stained by a runnel of greenish-grey ichor. This rapidly swelled to a stream as the tongue lashed from side to side, opening and spreading the wound.

The Queen's blood, if that's what it was, was welling up inside the hollow pole: it poured out of the end like a tap at first, but the pressure seemed to be increasing. Soon the foul-smelling fluid was jetting out with the force of a fire hose, spattering great swathes of thick gunge across the tunnel walls and ceiling while Lauren, still shrieking, was flung back and forth in the air.

Ben numbly wiped the goop from his eyes and just lay there, aghast.

After what seemed like an age, the shriek died down; the Queen's movements became less frantic. Lauren's side-to-side movements gradually slowed and the tongue dipped, losing strength, lowering its burden to the sloping tunnel floor. The torrent from the pole slowed to a trickle.

Both the Queen and Lauren were now still. Lauren was standing perhaps half a metre from where Jasmine had fallen. Her head was bowed, her face covered by her hair.

'Lauren?' Jasmine asked.

Slowly Lauren's head lifted. The eyes fixed on Jasmine, and when she saw what was in them she went cold.

Lauren's lips parted in a snarl.

'How . . . DARE you?' roared the Queen.

Lauren swung into the air once more. Her arms lifted from her sides. Then the Queen's new hands, which had entered the Pit Theatre and snuck into the tunnel behind, swarmed down on their prey.

Ben felt them all over him, climbing his chest under his shirt, wriggling in his hair. He leaped to his feet again, slapping and swatting at himself. *Jasmine!* he thought desperately. By the time he found her she was almost invisible under a clinging mound of crawlers but Ben dug in and grabbed her, hauling her upright, while, with his good hand, Robert did the same for Josh. Then the four of them stood there for a moment, quaking.

Ben held his breath, waiting for the bite, the hot needles sensation that would mean he was a slave again.

'You have . . . *hurt* me,' said the Queen slowly, disbelievingly. 'Me,' she repeated, through Lauren's mouth. 'Your Queen.'

'What can I say?' said a voice. 'I guess some people just don't like being told what to do.'

Ben turned.

'One last try?' added Josh. 'All together?'

'All together,' said Jasmine.

With that, the four of them grabbed the protruding end of the pole, and *shoved*.

The first person to fall again was Robert: his school shoes slipped on slime and he slammed to the floor on his back. Josh went next, as a fresh gout fountained out of the end of the pole and caught him square in the chest. Then Jasmine felt her knees buckling. The last person standing was Ben, his face a mask of determination, then he too sank to the ground, finally exhausted.

It was a desperate effort. Even with all four of them pushing the pressure on the pole was nothing compared to what they had managed to build up on their charge down the tunnel. Their improvised harpoon sank home about another ten centimetres, then stopped.

But it was enough.

Hugo felt a disgusting internal shifting sensation at the back of his head, then everything changed.

He was in the Barbican foyer. He seemed to be kneeling on the chest of a wide-eyed man that he was sure he'd never seen before, but his left hand was grasping the man's face, pinning the man's head to one side so his neck was bared. In Hugo's right hand, he was holding a crawler.

He stared at the man. Then he stared at the creature. The crawler's legs twitched once, then drooped. Hugo hurled it away with a spasm of disgust. He stood up, releasing the man, and looked around.

Between the feet of the surrounding crowd the Barbican carpet was dotted all over with inert crawler bodies, lying where they'd dropped. There were over a thousand people in the foyer, including assorted police, members of the armed forces, and other specialists. For another moment there was silence. Everyone was looking at each other. Everyone, like Hugo, was trying to assess what had happened, what they were doing there. Then the silence was broken by a rising clamour of confused voices.

The Queen gave a last, agonized, rippling shudder, then stopped moving. Supported only by the jutting pole, the wounded tongue lolled slackly. Released, Lauren toppled forward, landing face-down in the slime with a smack.

'We can't just leave her,' said Jasmine. 'Help her, someone!'

Ben and Josh did as she asked: they heaved Lauren up, supporting her between them. Every movement dislodged more of the tiny crawlers still caught on their clothes and hair. The creatures fell to the tunnel floor, legs upturned, lifeless.

'Right,' said Jasmine. 'Let's go.'

Lisa woke on the floor of the security room, alone. She had been dreaming. Or at least, she *thought* she'd been dreaming, but the dream had been about this room, the security room, so now she wasn't so sure. She had memories too: the memories were strange and blurry and frightening. The bruises on her arms, however, were very real. Lisa's mousey hair swung forward over her face as she stood up. She touched her stomach, and shivered. Then she saw that the door was open.

'This way to the exits, ladies and gentlemen!' said a megaphoned voice. *'Please proceed in an orderly fashion. Medical staff are on standby. The crisis is over. There's no cause for alar—'*

There was a distant *BOOM*, then a shuddering rumble that travelled through the whole building.

Samantha felt it in the soles of her shoes. Plenty of the adults in the foyer crowd obviously felt it too, because the crush around the Silk Street entrance suddenly intensified and, once again, the air filled with screams.

Sod this, thought Samantha, digging through with her elbows and hacking the shins of anyone who got in her way, *I'm out of here.*

'The countdown was . . . serious, then,' noted Josh as he and Ben heaved Lauren up to the first landing of the stairs from the Barbican's Pit level. 'How long . . . d'you think . . . we've got?'

'How . . . should I know?' Ben gasped back.

Crawlers crunched under his soles with every step. It was

hard to keep his footing without slipping, and Lauren was a lot heavier than she looked. Ben had reached the end of his string: his mind was numb. He had noticed the vibration in the floor, and knew what it meant: any second now the whole building was going to collapse around them all. He was so tired, he almost couldn't bring himself to care.

'Huh? Wossat?' said a voice from beside his ear. Then: 'Gerroff!'

Lauren was regaining consciousness.

'How are you feeling?' asked Jasmine. 'Can you stand?'

'Better yet,' said Josh, 'can you run?'

Lauren frowned groggily, then nodded. 'Think so. Yeah.'

'Then let's go,' Jasmine said again, not very calmly. 'Quick as you can, please, Lauren, because otherwise we're all going to die.'

But Ben was distracted.

When he set off up the stairs again, he would be around a corner; from where he was standing now, he could look back and take a last glance at the doors to the Pit Theatre, and the carpet of bodies.

Somewhere in the mass, past the upturned legs of a giant-size crawler at the bottom of the stairs, he saw movement.

BOOM. The rumbling under his feet became more pronounced.

'Ben!' said Jasmine.

Josh, Robert, even Lauren, had all gone ahead. But Jasmine was waiting for him.

Jasmine was *awesome*, Ben thought, again.

'Sorry,' he said. *Must have imagined it*, he told himself. He started off up the stairs behind her.

By the time they reached the upper foyer level it was empty. There was nothing between Ben and Jasmine and the Barbican's main entrance but the same straight stretch of carpet they'd failed to cross earlier. Lauren, Robert and Josh were already halfway there. Ben slogged on out into the deserted foyer behind Jasmine.

He wasn't too sure why they weren't dead already. Maybe blowing up a building was harder in real life than it was in the movies. He'd seen YouTube clips of demolitions so he had a rough idea of how they worked: if you wanted to knock down a building without damaging the surrounding area too much you set charges at different points, so that everything collapsed steadily inward on top of itself.

Rumble. When Ben and Jasmine reached the halfway point the foyer's lights flickered and went out. The air in Ben's labouring lungs took on a hot, smoky tang, thick with disturbed dust. He could still make out the revolving lights of the army and medical vehicles beyond the glass outside, so he pushed himself on towards them.

Now adults in protective gear just inside the entrance

were grabbing Josh, Lauren and Robert, bundling them out to safety. Now they had Jasmine – and a last, brave rescuer was beckoning frantically at him.

Just a few more steps, Ben thought with hysterical glee. They were actually going to get out of there! He could hardly believe it. They'd survived! They'd done it! They'd made it! They'd—!

Something massive swatted Ben in the back, knocking him flying. He heard no explosion but felt a sudden intense heat, then the world dissolved in a golden bloom of light.

Just a few more steps, Ben thought with hysterical glee. They were actually going to get out of there! He could hardly believe it. They'd survived! They'd done it! They'd made it! They'd—!

Something massive swatted Ben in the back, knocking him flying. He heard no explosion but felt a sudden intense heat, then the world dissolved in a golden bloom of light.

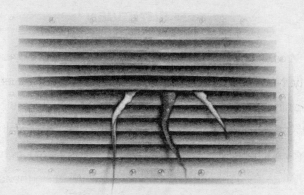

GREAT ORMOND STREET HOSPITAL FOR CHILDREN.
The Barrie Wing.

6:22 PM.

'So let me get this straight,' said the smartly dressed lady. 'You "harpooned" the alien queen with a scaffolding pole' – she grimaced – 'then you ran out of the Barbican Centre just before it exploded.'

'That's about the size of it,' said Ben, crossing his arms. 'Yeah.'

There were more details of course: after the amount of times he'd been over his statement Ben thought the lady should have known them as well as he did. But it had been a long night and he was starting to feel defensive. Not to mention frustrated and angry.

'Ben . . .' The lady pinched the bridge of her nose. 'I'll be straight with you. That's just about the most unlikely story I've ever heard.'

'*What?*' said Ben.

'It's true that the Barbican was destroyed, of course. And I suppose it's true, too, that we haven't completely ruled out all the possibilities as to why. But I'll tell you right now, I don't think anyone is considering . . . *aliens.*'

'What about the others?' asked Ben. 'What do they say?'

'You mean the other children who were with you?' The lady checked her notes. 'Yes, at first they corroborated your account. And the earlier parts of it, about "crawlers", and so forth' – she sneered – 'do seem to match up with the first statements we took from the adult witnesses – those who initially claimed to remember anything, of course.'

'Well?' said Ben.

'But everyone else but you has since *retracted* these statements,' the lady continued, with a small smile. 'After further questioning they admitted that this business with your "queen" creature just . . . wasn't how it happened. Ben,' she added, leaning forward on her chair, 'I think it's time you thought about doing the same.'

'Wait a second,' said Ben, confused. 'They . . . what?'

'Here's what we've told the press,' said the lady, shutting her file with a snap. 'Are you ready?'

She now held the file that contained Ben's story against her chest, her arms crossed in front of it. But from where Ben was lying, propped up on his hospital bed, the logo on the front of the file was perfectly readable: THE CORPORATION OF THE CITY OF LONDON, it said.

'At about seven forty-five last night,' the lady began, 'the Barbican was seized and taken over by persons unknown. Their identities remain a mystery at this time but there seems little doubt that these people were, in fact, terrorists.'

'Terrorists?' said Ben. 'That's the lamest excuse in the—'

'The terrorists sealed off the building,' the lady continued, interrupting him, 'and they then proceeded to use some means – most likely the air-conditioning – to flood the Barbican with a kind of *hallucinogen*. With the Barbican destroyed, no evidence of this mind-altering substance remains . . .'

'Hah,' said Ben.

'But it nonetheless seems to have been extremely potent. Civilian victims were so strongly affected that when police attempted to gain entrance to the Barbican, the civilians *attacked* them. A siege developed that lasted several hours. This, we assume, gave the terrorists time to set their explosives. Just before the bombs were detonated, however, the gas seems to have started wearing off. Emergency services were able to evacuate a large number of victims from the Barbican, including yourself and your . . . friends. But at least as many are still missing and, tragically, presumed dead. We can only assume those responsible for this atrocity were either caught in the blast . . . or they escaped.'

The lady sat back on her chair and gave Ben a smile that didn't reach her eyes. 'Ben,' she said, 'you seem like an intelligent young man – if a little too keen on video games, perhaps.'

Ben didn't smile back.

'Let me ask you a question. What would *you* find easiest to believe in – terrorists? Or – what was it, again? Oh yes: an *alien queen*, who controls people's minds?'

Ben was about to speak—

'Before you answer,' the lady interrupted again, 'I'd like you to consider one more thing.' She gestured at the door of the room. 'Your parents are out there in the passage. They're worried sick about you and they want to take you home. But a Corporation doctor is out there too, and he's waiting for my opinion before we decide what to do with you. Now . . .' She fixed Ben with a stare from her clear blue eyes. 'I can either say you're fine – that you will recover from your ordeal with no ill-effects and no memory of what really happened. Or we can send your parents home while we keep you here pending a full psychiatric evaluation.

'We can do that, you know,' she added silkily. 'The way you've been talking, I think that you could be a danger to yourself and to others. It would be irresponsible of me to allow you to be released while you still believe in things that are not . . . sensible.' She looked at him carefully. 'Do we understand each other?'

There was a pause.

Ben looked at the woman with the folder. He thought about the office he'd seen in the underground chamber, with the pictures on its walls of prime ministers and presidents.

'Well, Ben?' she asked. 'Which is it to be?'

Ben muttered something.

'What was that?'

'Terrorists,' said Ben.

'Good boy.'

THE SWATHAM ACADEMY FOR GIRLS.
A cubicle in the student toilets in the science block, two weeks later.

11:26 PM.

'I'm telling you,' Jasmine said into her phone, 'something weird is definitely going on. Samantha and Lauren are going around acting *exactly the way they were before* – like nothing even happened. Then, as if that wasn't weird enough, there's Lisa: today when I passed the school gates she was in the middle of a crowd. As I went by, all the girls around her turned to look at me. They smiled – all of them, all at once. Well?' she added. 'What does that remind you of, Ben?'

Ben's reply was hard to hear, almost drowned out as it was

by a passing group of boys behind him. Mobiles were still forbidden at his school: he was having to call Jasmine from a payphone.

Jasmine sighed. 'I'm sorry. I know you believe me. I know you do. But I just get so *frustrated*. It's like no one who was there wants to admit what happened – like they prefer the official version, because it's less scary. And you know what the worst thing is? Sometimes . . . I feel the same way.'

Jasmine bit her lip. 'Those squashed crawlers in the security room: we thought they were dead too,' she said. 'What if we didn't kill her, Ben? Because if she *did* escape, if she's out there right now taking more subjects, making more surrogates, *hatching* . . . whew. I'm not sure I even want to think about it myself.'

Jasmine listened to what Ben had to say. She smiled.

'Yeah,' she said softly. 'You watch yourself, too. Speak soon.' She blew him a kiss, pressed the button to end the call, and opened the cubicle door.

'Well, well,' said Samantha, who was standing outside. 'What have we here?'

For a moment Jasmine was so startled she couldn't reply.

The sudden jangle of the school bell for the end of morning break gave her the second she needed to collect herself.

'My private conversations are none of your business,' she said, and pushed past.

'Oh yeah?' crowed Lauren. 'And who do you think *you* are? Queen of Everything?'

Samantha and Lauren grinned at each other, then followed Jasmine out of the toilets. The door swung shut. The noise of the students in the corridor outside faded away. The only sound was the faint drip-dripping from one of the basins.

The dripping stopped. Then, with an effort, a thumbnail-sized creature pulled itself out of the tap.

It had five legs. It was not alone.

Oh, the children had hurt me, certainly. If I had not feigned death, Jasmine and the others might even have actually killed me. But once out of their sight, I was more than capable of limping to safety. Wounded but very much alive, I left the Barbican to its fate and took to the sewers.

My plan progresses well. Each hour brings fresh hatchings, and my hands now reach across this world. I control your leaders. I hide in the embraces of lovers and family; I crawl into your beds and take more of you as you sleep. Soon my present need for stealth will pass, for I will rule you completely.

You, reading these words now, a question: Are you quite certain you aren't mine already?

Check yourself. Find nothing. But remember: with those who might resist me I have learned to be less . . . direct. Perhaps you only feel what I allow you to feel. Perhaps the hand you raise to the back of your neck fails to detect the royal hand already upon you.

Prepare. My rule begins.

ACKNOWLEDGEMENTS

I'd like to take this chance to thank all the amazing young people I've met and spoken to over the last three years, whether at my events in schools, libraries and bookshops or via my websites. As I hope you can see from this book, your comments, questions and suggestions have a direct and inspiring effect on my writing. Thank you.

My thanks, too, to Kelly and Ruth for their awesome editorial acuity; to Penny and Gina for keeping faith; to Simon and Jack for their trusty (and terrifying) early draft reading skills – and, as ever, to my lovely girlfriend Laura, with all my heart.

On with the sinister masterplan!

All best wishes to you,

Sam

9th July 2009

TIM
DEFENDER OF THE EARTH
By **SAM ENTHOVEN**

He's big, he's moody, he has a
tail that could crush the Houses
of Parliament . . . and he's all that
stands between the Earth and total
destruction. (Oh, and he's actually
pretty nice . . . razor-sharp-car-
sized teeth notwithstanding).

TIM (that's Tyrannosaur: Improved Model) is
the product of a top-secret military experiment.

He forms an unlikely alliance with fourteen-year-old
Chris and his classmate, Anna, in order to save humanity
from the greatest threat it has ever known: Anna's father,
the brilliant but demented Professor Mallahide and
his growing swarm of vicious nanobats.

The stage is set for a spectacular showdown.
Who will prevail? The terrifying Professor Mallahide,
or TIM, DEFENDER OF THE EARTH . . . ?

ISBN: 978 0 552 55359 9